THE DISTORTIONS

THE DISTORTIONS

stories

Christopher Linforth

ORISON
BOOKS

Print ISBN: 978-1-949039-31-3
E-book ISBN: 978-1-949039-32-0

Orison Books
PO Box 8385
Asheville, NC 28814
www.orisonbooks.com

Distributed to the trade by Itasca Books
(952) 223-8373 / orders@itascabooks.com

Cover art by Vjenceslav Richter. Used with permission from the
Museum of Contemporary Art – Zagreb.

Manufactured in the U.S.A.

ORISON
BOOKS

Contents

for Sasha

The Distortions

The last time my great uncle shouted at his downstairs neighbor, he fired off a barrage of ethnic slurs, each successive curse deepening his Bosnian accent. My uncle was out on the balcony of his Zagreb flat. He spat the name Milošević and something about the war with the Serbs. I was fiddling with the loop antenna of his TV, trying to eliminate the white static and ghostly images of the war crimes tribunal. I couldn't hear much else of what was happening, so I went out to check on him. My uncle was standing awkwardly in his baggy brown suit, his body pressed against the balcony wall. His head was dipped, and drops of spittle hung from his bottom lip.

"Everything okay?"

My uncle didn't answer but waved me over.

"The TV's broken," I said.

"Forget about that, Adin." Back in America I went by Adam, which was not an accurate translation of my name, but the closest version I was comfortable with. "Come spit."

I came to his side and looked down. Another old man, dressed similarly to my uncle, gazed upward from the balcony below. "Got yourself a young lover!" yelled the man.

My uncle swiped the air. "Serbs," he said to me, "are the closeted ones."

This sort of conversation, which my uncle got into with most people, whatever their nationality, seemed representative of my short time in the former Yugoslavia, the country of my birth. Most of my family had escaped Bosnia in 1992 and moved to New York. I was three, an only child, one too young to understand what had caused us to leave. Now I was back, albeit two hundred and fifty miles from Sarajevo. So far I felt out of sorts with this place, and the balcony view of Communist-era tower blocks struck me as another depressing reminder that I missed my apartment in Crown Heights and my girlfriend, Laura. Beyond the concrete sprawl, across the Sava River, lay the old part of Zagreb. Deep in the clutter of terracotta-roofed buildings stood the Mirogoj Cemetery, the only landmark I had any interest in exploring.

My uncle leaned back over the wall and spat at his neighbor. Then he turned around and stuck a cigarette in his mouth. As he headed inside the flat, I waved to the man, mouthed an apology, and trailed my uncle back into the living room. My uncle fixed himself a drink and eased into his spot on the sofa. Fanned on the coffee table in front of him were old family letters and black-and-white photographs of farms somewhere in Bosnia.

"I don't know why I have to go," he said.

"You have no one here to look after you."

"What is there for me in America?"

"Family."

"The good ones died in the massacre."

I didn't know what to say to that.

I had flown into Zagreb a few weeks before, ostensibly to help my great uncle prepare for a move to America, to reunite him with relatives who had fled before the destruction of Sarajevo. I had been appointed by my grandmother. Over cups of strong black coffee, in her Brighton Beach house, she sketched me a portrait of her older brother: an exile in Zagreb, ex-Orthodox, cantankerous, a heavy drinker, always lonely. I told her I had work but hid that it was freelance content writing—and poorly paid, at that. She pressed me several times, feeding me slices of ružice and saying it was my responsibility as the oldest of her grandchildren. Though I was almost thirty, I had shirked a lifetime of responsibility, a privilege of my upbringing in America. I remembered little from those blurry childhood years in Bosnia, and I feigned resistance, swirling my hand in the air and mentioning deadlines with a host of online men's lifestyle magazines. In truth, I was looking for a break. My life in Brooklyn had reached a nadir: crippling student loan payments and a girlfriend who was eternally disappointed in my profiles of hip neighborhoods and men with dad bods, not to mention my weekly column on bros and their cats. Laura worked in publishing, a literary imprint of some international behemoth. She was not incorrect in her critical judgment of my work or in her assertion that I was depressed. In my spare time I visited cemeteries, spending hours finding the saddest gravesites. This was not a morbid practice, exactly. It felt, at least to me, like an attractive force at work, the universe pulling me toward others who were worse off.

It had begun in Green-Wood, a month or two before, while searching for my grandfather's grave. Along a bluestone path, I stumbled across a pair of matching headstones: a married couple. The husband had died in 1977, at the age of eighty-eight, while the wife, miraculously, appeared to be alive. Her death date had not been chiseled into the blank section of granite. Born at the start of the twentieth century, Mary Simonson was now one hundred and nineteen years old. I imagined she lived in Queens, sprightly as ever.

After this I visited Woodlawn and Cypress Hill. I even took the train out to Calvary. Hours of traipsing around brought me temporary death notices staked in the earth, never replaced with anything else; babies dying at just a few days old, their plush toys dirty and rotted; a man crying by a fresh mound of dirt. Yet, in drunken moments, when I would regale Laura with my latest cemetery discoveries or talk again of Mary Simonson, she would state bluntly, "Adam, she's dead. She's been forgotten. They all have."

My uncle frowned on my international calls to Laura. Even when I offered to pay him, he told me no, that would be American. I telephoned her late in the night, around two or three a.m., knowing she was six hours behind. She always sounded distant, uninterested, aside from her opinion that I should have brought my cellphone with me. When I suggested I wanted a return to a pre-digital era, she told me I was backward.

"Perhaps we shouldn't even talk," she said.

"I could send you letters."

"I meant that we should take a break."

"Is that what you want?"

"Neither of us has ever said we're in love."

"There hasn't been a right moment."

"Adam," she said, sounding exasperated, "what do you imagine it says on my headstone?"

"You're not dead."

When I said this, I heard a muffled sound on the other end of the line. It could have been a man's laugh or the traffic outside of her apartment. I wondered what I was doing thousands of miles away. In the six months we had been dating, our relationship had never really been tested. We'd had a couple of fights over my career choices, the fact she had coveted a financially stable partner. Like her, her exes had attended Ivies. Brad (Cornell) was a stockbroker. Noah (Princeton) also did something on Wall Street. Oliver (Brown) was a successful sculptor. The list went on. I had gone to a CUNY school (York College) and studied journalism. Perhaps she was slumming it with me.

"Is someone else there?"

"I can't do this now," she said. "I have to go."

After Laura hung up, I held the receiver next to my ear until my uncle came out from his room and told me the conversation was over.

I slept in the smaller of my uncle's two bedrooms, staring each night at the stacks of boxes I had to sort out. Daylight revealed bundles of newspapers and disorderly research documents in manila folders. I knew from my grandmother that he had been a journalist in Sarajevo for a few years, but I had assumed that he'd worked on local stories, inspecting minutes from bureaucratic council meetings and election results. It surprised me that he had done any investigative reporting at all.

In his files from the 1990s, I came across a dozen or more pieces on the creation of a new Serb territory in northern and eastern Bosnia. His byline for the newspaper used his complete name: Dženan Petar Handanović. Throughout his writing his distrust of Republika Srpska was evident. There were few mentions of the Siege of Sarajevo or the massacre in Srebrenica. Either he had been reluctant to describe the madness around him, the killing of his friends and colleagues, or he had destroyed the articles, leaving the events to reside only in his memory.

Our written labor, fashioned with speedy, workmanlike prose, was one thing I thought we had in common, but the arc of his career widened the gulf between us. According to his nightly drunken ramblings on the balcony, it was during this period of his life that he had learned English over hotel bar drinks with British and American reporters and from his ritual of listening to the BBC World Service before bed. I was just a child at that time; my parents evacuated us to New York when I was barely three. During conversations with my grandmother she would mention her brother back in Croatia now and again, usually when a member of our family had died. To me, my uncle was just another relative from the old country, a man I would never meet.

As the days ticked by, I remained in the flat sorting through my uncle's possessions while he completed some business in the city, an accountant here, an ex-colleague there. He rarely went into detail. On his return his breath always reeked of hard liquor and cigarette smoke. He spent most evenings on the balcony bickering with the neighbor. Though I had a tenuous grasp of the language, I could decipher some of his words. He railed at the man about the now-defunct Yugoslav soccer league, about fouls by Red Star players who were now surely dead. They argued over scores and offside goals and drifted into a dispute over the death count in Srebrenica. My uncle said the number of murdered ran into the tens of thousands; the neighbor countered it was closer to a couple of hundred. Then he bellowed out a hearty laugh and asked where my uncle's young concubine was, that he could show him—me!—a good time.

This sort of thing hampered my progress in preparing my uncle for his move to America. One evening, I decided to discuss with him the itinerary's condensed timeline. My uncle was dozing in his rattan chair on the balcony, his feet up on a beer crate. Beside him sat a bottle of šljivovica, a mug he used as an ashtray, and a stack of papers underneath. His thick body was leaned back into the chair, his eyelids fluttering, his throat producing a comical snore. From somewhere below the balcony a loud voice shouted for Petar. My uncle seemed too inebriated to respond. I clutched the flight reservation, a little apprehensive about reminding him we were leaving in a week.

I knocked on the glass door. "What are we going to do with all your boxes?"

My uncle opened one eye. He saw me through the door and cupped his ear.

I came out onto the balcony. "The boxes," I said.

"Never mind those. Have a drink."

I waved him off, and he tweezed a cigarette stub out of the mug. He wedged it between his lips and lit the end. He exhaled a column of smoke into the air. Before long we heard orchestral music blare from below. It sounded to me like Serbia's national anthem.

"I'm ignoring the idiot neighbor," he said. "He's taking it personally."

"Soon you won't have to worry about him anymore."

"We'll see." He pointed to the makeshift coaster beneath his mug. "My passport is no good."

I retrieved his passport and inspected the blood-red

cover. The gold emblem of Yugoslavia dominated the front: wheat encircled six flaming torches, a red star at the top. I flipped through the thick pages to his picture: a rotund face, cleanly shaven, hair dark and greased in a side parting. The date revealed the passport had expired twenty years ago. "We'll get you another one."

My uncle made a face. "No, you don't understand." He motioned for me to sit on the concrete floor, but I kept standing, sensing something was up. "Yugoslavia's over," he said. "Just a Bosnian one works now."

I knew this, of course, but the magnitude of what he was confessing took a moment to register. He had no passport, no visa, no legal means to be anything other than a tourist in America. Back at my grandmother's house, I had been under the impression he was ready to go. Perhaps this had been part of my grandmother's plan, I considered now: to stash him in her house illegally, and let him live out the remainder of his life in a back bedroom or darkened basement.

I leaned against the balcony wall. My shoulders slumped, and a chill seeped up my back, half-numbing my thoughts. Behind my uncle, the city lights blinked in the cold air. I could see a blacked-out area, which was the Mirogoj Cemetery. I thought again of Laura and how I had left things. I had to get back to America, one way or another. Still, part of me had not yet given up on taking my uncle. This passport setback could be overcome. "We're flying to New York either way," I said. "I want to make that clear."

My uncle flicked his cigarette over the side of the balcony. "You just want to see your woman."

"It's not that."

"Of course it is. What am I going to do in your country?"

"Spend time with your sister. Catch up with her."

"I'm already caught up: she's American."

The music broke off. My uncle smiled and poured me a healthy dose of šljivovica. I took it gladly and cradled the glass in my hands. I studied the clear liquid glinting in ambient light, then knocked the brandy back.

That night I called Laura. I wanted to ask if she would visit my grandmother, who, almost deaf, rarely answered her telephone. Everything was supposed to be arranged, my role merely to be a physical aid to my uncle, a pair of hands to guide him to the plane. In fogged drunkenness I dialed Laura's number and waited, the ring on the line a shout into the void.

The next morning, my uncle and I set off for the Bosnia and Herzegovina Embassy. We rode the tram across the Sava River into Zagreb. We alighted at Britanski Trg and walked up Pantovčak. My uncle stopped a couple of times to catch his breath. While he waited he lit a cigarette, explaining the nicotine opened up his lungs.

Past a series of expensive houses, we located the arched gate of the embassy. Outside, a handful of wizened men and women waited their turn to enter the modern villa. We shuffled along the sidewalk as the line of people slowly dissipated. Once we were admitted, we were escorted to a processing room furnished with rows of cantilever chairs. Most were already occupied, so we seated ourselves in the corner, near a brightly lit hallway. I recognized the subjects of three government portraits spanning the far wall: the current triad of the Bosnia-Herzegovina presidency. Bizarre to Americans, if they knew of it, and almost all did not: the country operated on a collective system, a three-person head of state.

I pointed out the odd state of affairs to my uncle, but he just retrieved his pack of cigarettes. He plucked one out and grinned at me. I had told him something he already knew. The postwar decision that Croats, Serbs, and Bosniaks would be equally represented in the government was common knowledge over here. As he sparked his lighter, a security guard came over and informed my uncle he couldn't smoke.

"I suppose I should practice for America," my uncle said to me. "I hear that country loves its Puritan heritage."

"All countries have a checkered past."

My uncle pinched my arm. "Listen to me: I abhor the pretense of getting along. Serbs took my home, killed my friends, my cousins, my son."

I hadn't heard of the existence of my uncle's son before. I knew about his wife who died of breast cancer several years ago. But a son? I wondered if my grandmother knew. Even at our last meeting, she had just said her brother lived alone. Nothing else.

"I'm sorry," I said.

"You didn't kill him."

"Uncle, no one told me you had a son."

"Why would they?"

"Tell me about him."

My uncle stared at the portraits, seemingly trying to divine an answer that would satisfy me. "We had him late in life," he said, his voice cracking. "And then not for very long."

"Does the family know?"

"What do they care? They survived. They went to a better place. Davud did not." He went across to the chairs facing a large digital clock. He averted eye contact with me, drummed his fingers on his folder of documents, and stared at the clock. When my uncle's name was announced over the speaker system, he got up to meet a well-dressed woman, and he followed her down the hall.

I switched to my uncle's seat in a show of familial solidarity. In the residual warmth of his chair, I thought about his dead son. Had Davud died in the shelling of Sarajevo? Or someplace else? I wondered where he was buried or if a memorial to him existed. Mass graves were all over Bosnia, in Prijedor and Foča and all along the border with Serbia. Soldiers executed boys who'd once been their young neighbors and fellow citizens. I tried to forget all of this. But I couldn't. Each time an androgynous voice on the speaker system summoned people to the hallway, the names sounded to me like those of the dead. Men and women drifted down the hall, vanishing into a series of rooms. In a bid to distract myself from my darker thoughts, I glanced through some magazines from a nearby coffee table, wondering if I could write for these publications. My uncle could translate, transposing my fluffy travel pieces on Mostar into hard-hitting exposés of political corruption, lifting the veil on the former Yugoslavia's war crimes.

Reveling in this absurdity, I attempted to memorize the names of those paged over the speaker system:

Bilal Gudelj

Emin Alić

Lalja Uma Jahić

Harun Jahić

Miloje Bjelić

Andrej Đalović

Besima Kopanja

Dženan Petar Handanović

I could remember no more. The number of people, both alive and dead, rendered the project futile, beyond my capacity to empathize. I concentrated on my uncle's immediate problem. We were too pressed for time to get a US visa of any sort. I prayed my uncle would be issued an emergency passport. Perhaps if he had bank statements and a return ticket, he would be let into America for a brief stay. My job would be done, my grandmother pleased, and I could work on rebuilding my relationship with Laura.

The last time I saw Laura we were in her loft apartment in Williamsburg. I made her dinner—a simple spaghetti carbonara—and she provided the wine. The conversation during our meal halted after I mentioned my upcoming trip to Croatia. She fell silent, thumbed her cellphone a couple of times. She said she was just checking the weather.

I realized now I should have asked her to come with me. Perhaps if she had seen the former Yugoslavia for herself, she would have understood me better and not been so concerned with my career or where I went to school. For years I had minimized my Bosnian heritage—any guilt downplayed to friends who had asked about my family escaping the war. I had seldom spoken to Laura about my childhood, about what my family had gone through. As a result, there was little doubt she thought I couldn't trust her.

After several hours, my uncle emerged, red-faced. He had removed his jacket and wrenched his necktie loose.

"They need my birth certificate," he said. "They don't believe who I am."

"That can't be right. Let me talk to them."

"No. I'm leaving," he said.

I shouted my uncle's name, but he disappeared through the doorway.

Back at the flat, I telephoned my grandmother, eager for her advice. I tried to reach her several times, but she never answered. I considered getting hold of my parents, who lived in St. Louis, or one of my friends in Brooklyn. Eventually I rang Laura at her Midtown office.

"You shouldn't call me here," she said.

"I need your help."

"We're on a break," she said. "I thought I made that clear."

"It's my grandmother." I could hear Laura hold her breath. "Can you check on her?"

"Is she sick?"

"No, she's not picking up. I just need her to call me."

"Fine," she said. "I'll do it. But please don't contact me here again."

All night I waited by the telephone stand for my grandmother's call. Slouched against the wall, I wondered if Laura had followed through with my request. She wasn't the type to flake. In all the time we had been dating, she had been the levelheaded one, the arranger of movie dates and brunches with her friends, the scheduler of when we could get together. Perhaps it was unfair of me to ask her. We were still in that nebulous post-breakup phase of trying to disentangle our lives from each other.

Before my uncle went to bed, he handed me a cup of coffee. He told me I was wasting my time, that he and his sister didn't get along very well. "Barely said a word to her in years," he said. His attitude did not stop me from sleeping by the telephone that night. Even for a day afterward, I hunkered down, desperate to hear from my grandmother.

By the time I conceded that I would have to organize my uncle's paperwork by myself a couple of days later, he had fallen ill. His face had turned wan and gray, and his cough, which I had not noticed at first, hacked at his throat. My uncle blamed a touch of flu and said he would go easy on the cigarettes. I went out and bought him some cough syrup and painkillers. At an internet café, I confirmed that my uncle would require a birth certificate to get his new passport, and to accomplish that he would have to travel to his hometown of Višegrad in Republika Srpska.

That afternoon, I ignored my uncle's protests and brought him aboard the train at Glavni Kolodvor. He seemed sullen as we seated ourselves in the carriage. He smoked and said if he were caught, the conductor could kick him off. For a couple of hours we sat in cough-punctuated silence. Outside, a torrential downpour thrashed the fields and farmhouses. Droplets clung to the glass and formed silver rivulets against the blur of gray countryside. Only when the train rattled across the border into Bosnia did my uncle glance out the window. The rain had let up to a drizzle, and I noticed his body had tightened.

"I don't know why we're bothering," he said. "We'll never make that flight."

"I'll reschedule. Or buy a new ticket."

"You make a lot of money back in America?"

I didn't want to admit that this was hardly the case.

"Enough," I replied.

"Any children?"

"No. My work takes up all my time."

"But someday? With that woman you call?"

"Maybe."

"I could have gone to New York all those years ago," he said. "I could have taken Elena and Davud with me. But I stayed. I wrote for the newspaper—let the world know what was happening."

"I'm glad you did."

"America didn't listen. Not for years."

I assured my uncle that he had done the right thing, but he shook his head. "Davud should have lived," he said. I had no answer for his pain. He had carried this burden with him for decades, and it struck me that my grandmother had somehow sensed his regret and known how to help him. She had positioned me—a stand-in for Davud—to be an incentive for his new life in America. I suspected to my uncle, though, I bore little resemblance to his son.

Before long the train stopped at the station in Brčko. We exited as quickly as we could, and were waved through border control for our connecting bus. Once aboard, my uncle turned away from me in his new seat and shut his eyes.

The bus pulled into Višegrad late that night. We caught a taxi to the hotel in the quiet part of town. French Tricolor flags festooned the colonnaded entrance of The Hotel Paris. Behind the front desk, a young man with finely shellacked hair and a pristine concierge jacket, whose name badge read Tarik, greeted us with a stilted "Bonjour." His French soon died away during check-in and he directed us up the stairs. Our room had several soft-focus photographs of Parisian streets. A large black-and-white print of the Eiffel Tower hung above the single bed. My uncle sat on the edge and joked that his neighbor must have made the reservation.

"He's a true romantic," I replied. A bulky television set sat in the corner. I wiped dust from the screen and pushed the channel buttons. Static washed over a flickering picture. I jiggered a tangle of cords at the back. Grainy images of people appeared and disappeared on the screen.

"Turn it off. We don't have sitcoms with coffee and young, stupid people," he said.

I laughed inwardly at his description of nineties television. I was sure half of his negative opinions about America came from old reruns. "I'm looking for a show about three middle-aged men and one woman, petty squabbles and hijinks."

"Adin, I don't know what you're talking about."

"You have decades of bad shows to look forward to."

"I should just stay here."

"Sure, die in this bed," I said.

I switched off the television and went downstairs to the lobby. I purchased a cheap phonecard from Tarik at the front desk, then slipped across to the telephone booth. I tucked myself inside the glassed-in vestibule; the overhead light blinked erratically. I examined the phonecard's elaborate instructions and dialed a long string of numbers.

A strange woman's voice answered. "Who?" she said.

"Adam."

"Oh. You're that guy."

"Can I speak to Laura?"

"She's not here," the woman said. "She's gone."

"Tell Laura to call me. The number is…" I glanced at the telephone case. Inside the dial, where the number should have been, sat an inlay of blank plastic. The line crackled.

Voices echoed, the words unintelligible.

"The Hotel Paris," I shouted.

"What? I can't understand what you're saying."

"She was loved," I said. "That's what it will say on her headstone."

I heard the familiar click of a receiver being replaced.

I dialed the number a second time, but a recorded voice stated the card had run out of credit. I considered buying another phonecard on the off chance my grandmother would answer, but decided against it. At the front desk, I quizzed Tarik about a place I could get a drink. He shook his head, then raised his finger for me to wait a moment. He went to the back room and returned with an unlabeled bottle and two glasses and poured us each a shot. "Živjeli," he said. I cheersed him back. After we downed our spirit, I asked about the records office and he fished out a town map from beneath the desk. The hundredth-generation photocopy veined distortions in the topography: smudged landmarks, conglomerated roads, faint vestiges of Cyrillic. Tarik looked up the address in the directory and scoured the map, ringing a gray square as my destination.

My uncle and I skipped breakfast in the morning. The truth was neither of us wanted to talk to the other. Sleeping beside him in the same bed, I had heard all the noisy protestations of his decrepit body. Aches slipped noisily from his mouth. His jerks and flinches blips on his circadian rhythm.

Leaving the hotel, Tarik passed me a note. "A poor transcription, I'm afraid," he said. "I could hardly hear the woman." Tarik's bad handwriting was further complicated by his use of Cyrillic. I stuffed the piece of paper in my pocket as my uncle approached. We made our way to the records office using the map, which proved to be out-of-date, and backtracked several times, finally asking for directions.

The squat limestone building had a small brass plaque denoting its bureaucratic function. My uncle studied the engraved words. Then he turned around to face the other side of the street. "A last cigarette. Then I'm quitting," he said.

As he fussed with his lighter, I unfurled the slip of paper. I asked my uncle to translate.

My uncle held the slip of paper close to his face and squinted. "I can't read this." He pressed the note into my hand and finished off his cigarette.

Inside the building, my uncle and I strode over to a man in a dour gray suit seated behind a metal-frame desk. The man lowered his newspaper, scrutinized my New York driver's license, and recorded my name in the logbook. He eyed my uncle's expired passport with suspicion. He informed us the registrar was away but that we could look by ourselves. "To get a copy of your birth certificate," he said flatly, "you have to locate your birth record." He led us down a few steps into a basement and through to a windowless room. Floor-to-ceiling shelves held hundreds of volumes.

"It's all yours," he said, and left.

My uncle and I split up to search the room. The records were divided in a manner I couldn't understand. Unlike my freelance work, this research would take time, and I could imagine Laura pointing out the benefits of digitized archives. I wished she had come here with me, but I doubted she ever liked me enough to visit this war-torn nation. Still, I contemplated how she would approach this task: she was methodical and organized, qualities she said I needed if I were to get my writing career on track. I started at the back row. I traced my finger over the books and took a few down, riffling through each to see if it was the correct one. Names filled each page, thousands of people I once shared a homeland with. I had left all of these men and women behind. I kept reading, incanting the names under my breath. Each person seemed to be part of a sprawling family tree. I lost track of time as I worked through the volumes, only waking from my self-induced trance to hear my uncle shouting.

"Adin," my uncle said as I joined him. "This is it." He lugged the book to a carrel basking in overhead fluorescent light. He thumbed through the pages. The closer he got to his birthdate the more excited he became. Then my uncle seemed puzzled. A thick strip of torn paper edges poked out like an inner spine. "The records have been taken," he said. "I'm not here." My uncle left the carrel and came back with the 1992 volume and repeated his search. A similar number of pages had been ripped from that book. "Davud's gone."

"What does this mean?" I asked.

"That we were fools to come here."

My uncle headed for the exit. I barely caught up to him as he dashed up the steps. As he swept past the man at the desk, my uncle muttered a few words. I stopped and complained about the missing records. "My uncle, his son, have been erased," I said. "The pages are gone."

"Your uncle fought on the wrong side." The man returned to his newspaper.

Outside, my uncle stood bent over, his breaths wheezy. His face had drained of color. "Just give me a minute."

"Are you alright?"

"Let me catch my breath."

I flagged down a taxi, and my uncle agreed to get in. We started off for the hotel. The driver was listening to the news on the radio, muttering to himself about the war crimes tribunal. My uncle fidgeted with the cuffs of his jacket, then removed it and folded it on his lap. Then my uncle jerked forward and asked the driver to circle back to a farm on the outskirts of town. "We're taking a detour," he said to me.

My uncle directed the driver. We crossed the bridge over the Drina River and took a back road that weaved through farmland for several miles. Acres of hilly fields crested against a forest. Sunrays broke through the clouds. With the light at our backs, the mountains appeared on the horizon. Serbia lay on the other side.

"This is it," my uncle said.

The driver pulled over. Down a mud track sat a farmhouse, the roof collapsed, the windows blown out. The building fronted an old potato field choked with ragweed. I was instantly reminded of my uncle's black-and-white photographs, though the scene before us looked desolate now. My uncle opened the taxi door and climbed out. I asked the driver to wait and chased after my uncle.

We hiked up the track and cut into the field. My uncle migrated to the far corner. He stared at the patch of ground for a while. I figured Davud was buried here, his small body wrapped in a plastic sheet, something simple and quick, so that my uncle could have evacuated the town that night. There was no memorial, no headstone, no childhood toy.

"This is my first time back," he said.

"There should be something here."

He knelt and sieved some dirt through his hand. "We remember. That is what's important." He raised his arm, and

I helped him back to his feet.

As we got back to the taxi, my uncle said, "I lied to you before. The note said something like, *I'm glad you two are alright.*"

It was unclear if that vague sentiment had come from my grandmother or Laura. In that moment, it didn't matter very much. My uncle patted the driver's shoulder. The taxi drove on and dropped us a little later outside of the hotel.

A light was on in an anteroom just off from the lobby. Tarik was sitting at a round table with his bottle of homemade spirit. His greased hair was slightly matted and his top shirt buttons were undone. He saw us and beckoned us over.

My uncle collapsed in a chair. "Petar," he said.

Tarik gestured to his name badge next to the bottle. "They wanted me to go by Jean. But I fought back."

My uncle smiled. "Glad you did."

Tarik nodded, then fetched two more glasses. He poured shots for us all. He raised his drink, and my uncle and I did the same.

"Santé," said my uncle.

Tarik laughed. "The owners of this hotel have never been to France."

"Nevertheless," my uncle said, pointing over Tarik's shoulder, "I appreciate the idea." Pinned above a set of fire regulations was a poster reproduction of a French Revolution-era trio of women. They wore white skirts and striped jackets, their headscarves a circus of blue, white, and red. Below the women's feet it said: Liberté, Égalité, Fraternité.

"Adin is from America," noted my uncle.

"I know," said Tarik. "His country honors the same

principles."

"It's far from perfect," I said. I sipped my drink. I felt a strong burn of alcohol on my throat but hid the eye-watering sensation.

My uncle drained his glass. "Adin has a woman there."

"Maybe," I said.

"Still, I might move to America."

"Then we should toast," I said, "to your journey."

Tarik poured us all another, and we clinked our glasses. We drank into the night, the three of us, sharing the bottle from one mouth to another. At some point long past midnight, Tarik and my uncle slipped deep into conversation about the old days. I imagined I could understand exactly what they were saying, and when my uncle asked if I was ready, I said that I was.

brb

Sophie: When you return, ignore what I have typed above. It was a quote, depending on the source, from Immanuel Kant or Mark Twain or Bertrand Russell, which I lifted from a factoid-conglomeration website and passed off as my own words. But the dictum barely conveys what I was trying to tell you.

So let me try again.

Philosophy can answer only a limited number of life's questions. Really it is an apparatus for considering how to live and how to treat others. You taught me this. Next to me now at my computer sits a handsome edition of Nietzsche's collected works and a German-to-English dictionary. I purchased both shortly after we first spoke online. When you told me you were learning German to read Nietzsche in the original, I was impressed, whether or not you ultimately discovered the purity of his thought. Who can say what "ewige Wiederkunft des Gleichen" actually means?—the words are just black marks on a page.

Perhaps this is the problem. Through IM, we speak to each other every night with similar black marks. They mean more to me than Nietzsche or any writers of his kind. But still, words are not enough. I need to see you and hear you speak. This is not a case of low self-esteem or high school ennui—it is because of certain events in my life. I graduate from my gimnazija soon, and I am at a loss what to do next. Both of my brothers attended the medical school at Sveučilište u Zagrebu, and my father expects the same of me. I know you think me to be wise and older than my years, but I am not. I doubt myself every day. Becoming a doctor will help others. I only want to help you.

But you need to act.

For I believed you when you said you would visit me from Winter Park, or would plan a trip to Italy with your parents, then sneak away onto the ferry to Dubrovnik. We were going to meet there, stay in a luxurious hotel overlooking a private beach—the sand imported from the Sahara, the waves of the Adriatic slowly eroding the shore. Imagine it: Across the sea your mother and father stand on the terracotta-tiled balcony, at a loss to know where you have gone. They speak to the police in their guidebook Italian, attempting to convince the ispettori their seventeen-year-old daughter would not just run off: *She's a good girl, a Christian, a straight-A student and valedictorian. In the fall she's attending Princeton. She's going to be a philosophy major. You must believe us. She reads all the time: Balzac, Camus, Kierkegaard. There's a poster of Simone de Beauvoir above her bed. She's never had a boyfriend or shown any inclination to want one. Please, you must find her. She loves books, her friends, her dog and hamster. Not boys or makeup or celebrity culture or internet pornography.*

You were going to be with me. I had it all planned. Our conversations over the last six months have shown me how I can please you. Croatia is not that different from Florida. Sunlight warms the old Communist concrete of Mamutica and the other apartment towers dotted throughout Novi Zagreb. Guns from our wars are lost in lofts and basements or out on the hills, close to long-forgotten landmines and bodies buried in the wet earth. Like your Confederates, Chetnik Serbs still curse at us and say we are the aggressor, the destroyer of the Republic.

Ha!

Disney World sits a few miles from you, but the visitors here in Zagreb speak French or German and disdain Americans and anything supersized or related to President Bush and his warmongering. And let us not forget Britain and its tourists, who plague my country's historic attractions and drink too much beer and vomit a dark broth in the street. They still strut around as if they rule an empire. Once you are here we will shout *1776!* at them, though the year means something different in this country.

Hand-in-hand, we will walk along the ancient city walls and wend our way down to the harbor. Sailboats bob in the water and gulls squawk overhead. Bare-chested fishermen mend their nets. Every scene is a picture postcard. There is a café that serves bijela kava and slices of orehnjača. I already see us basking in the sun, using the dialectical method to reason through your religiosity, your adherence to family. You do not miss your church or your parents or your TV. You do not even have to say you will be back after *The Simpsons* or *Arrested Development*, or that you will be delayed because of the new boy two houses down. Both of us finally together, sitting in the café, everything is understood between us.

When the sugar and caffeine push us on, and we leave, we admit our love. It is the first time you feel something since your sister died. The feeling is greater than your loss, greater than your discovery after the funeral of the pocket-sized book of Nietzsche's quotes, and greater than your curiosity at her annotations. She barely grasped his version of the eternal recurrence, a repeating of particles, in one form or another, through time. But you are the smarter girl, the one willing to grow, physically and mentally, and I have observed this since our first meeting in the chatroom. From our initial exchanges about your sister's suicide and the hypocrisy of Catholicism all around you, our friendship grew over the months. Our typed chat became our bond, our invocations of love. And so, here we are outside the café: one Floridian girl and one Croatian gospodin. In the street we listen to the busker strumming his guitar, singing the wrong words to an eighties hit, and after you drop him a few lipa, we move on to a seafood restaurant and drink white wine and listen to the flat sounds of the piano drifting across the dining room. The waiter asks you if want dessert and you giggle. And I laugh, knowing what is on your mind. It will be our private joke—the whole day we've had, and the night to come.

Afterward we retire to the hotel, and you close the drapes and say you cannot even remember who your parents are. They are just two people, like us, locked in their own world. *What do the words "mother" and "father" even mean?* you ask. You ponder this question as you inspect the room and forget you were searching for an answer when you find the Bible in the nightstand drawer. Flipping through the pages, you pretend not to be drawn to the packets of gummy bears and a chilled six-pack of honeyed lager on top of the television cabinet. I open two of the beers and hand you one bottle. You toss the Bible into the wire trash basket and guzzle the cold beer greedily. We jump into bed and roll in the sheets and kiss and take snapshots with my new digital camera and post them online as a middle finger to your parents and your "friends" who told you to stop IMing me. It would be funny, and funnier when we joke about a threesome with a gummy bear, and I prop one up in your navel and shake hands with its gelatin paw, then run my fingertip over its swollen abdomen and underneath to the smoothed-out area where no genitals dwell. You laugh, flashing your orthodontic braces, but then press your lips together, self-conscious of your slight underbite. We kiss. We make love—lose our virginities. We hold each other afterward in the warm mist of the shower and pretend no one else exists in the world. It is our shared solipsistic fantasy.

People will not understand our relationship. I know that, and you should too.

We are only three years into a new millennium, and I feel like I preferred the last. You were right: I am an old soul, more at home with the bureaucratic mechanisms of socialism than the benefits of neo-liberalism and the rage and grief surrounding the Twin Towers attack. Over here you would be safe. Over here you have me and my home. You will not need your cellphone or Mac or iPod. Over here we will listen to live bands and eat real food. Over here we have better dining options than Chili's and Bonefish Grill and EVOS and Bahama Breeze. You will be healthy over here. You will not have to take your Xanax or your Adderall or steal your mother's OxyContin. You will not have to worry about receiving money from her or your father, or being screwed over by your teachers or "friends," or explaining your guilt over your sister's suicide to your therapist and your priest. You will not have to go to Mass. You can throw away your nickel prayer beads and the Catholic Bible presented to you on your confirmation. God is dead—we both know this. I will look after you. I will take possession of your philosophy books, and your childhood encyclopedias and almanacs, and your sister's hairbrush and her journal hidden in an old cigar box. We will transport your dog and hamster. We won't forget them. I cannot, even now. In the webcam image of you holding your pets, you cup each animal close to your breasts to hide your beauty. But you cannot see your white cotton tank top ride up on the waistband of your baby-blue Lycra shorts, exposing a sliver of pale midriff.

Your pictures cause me to weep.

If you come here, what am I to do? The photograph of the face I sent you is not mine. I searched for *handsome Eastern European teenager* and found my alter ego on the second page of the image results. His dark eyes and hair, the small scar on his jawline. He is perfect, even down to the exquisite musculature of his neck, and his black hair, shorn on both sides, the top slicked back. I like to think he is a younger version of myself. To be seventeen and in love—why does it feel so long ago, but so close to my heart?

The reason is you.

Sophie. Oh, Sophie. My Sofia. I wish I were that teenage boy. I wish I lived in Zagreb and were just about to graduate. I wish I could be a doctor or turn down medical school for you. I am for all intents and purposes someone else: a father of two girls, a husband to Marta, a civil servant, an owner of a small flat and a decrepit Yugo. There is no point telling you where I actually live, or the day-to-day of my life here. It is a boring existence. All of your favorite philosophers would have hated this version of living, considered the limitations of my life a death sentence. My hair is the color of pewter and folds of fat rib my neck and belly. Sometimes my breaths are shallow, but I am fine below the waist. Before you denounce me, know that I have devoured *The World as Will and Representation* and *Republic* and *Prolegomena to Any Future Metaphysics*, all for you.

I hope these messages are enough, Sophie. For all we have is language, our sounds and our meanings and our thoughts. We both know the quote—whoever said it first— is unsatisfactory, like all utterances. Blame Wittgenstein and his *Tractatus*, if you allow me one last joke. Now all I can hope is that the sentiment comes across, and that before you block my account, you will forgive me.

Men of the World

The first noise to interrupt Vedran's sunbathing on the back lawn was the sound of the hallway telephone. As soon as he had dismissed the call as unimportant, his wife stood at the back step, the receiver cradled to her chest, trilling an order to pick up Jakov from the train station. At his spot overlooking the lake, Vedran leaned into his lawn chair and swirled the remains of rakija in his glass. Even though he had not once met his wife's rich cousin, he had never cared for the sound of him. Jakov had left the country just after the war had broken out. Vedran drained his plum brandy and lobbed the glass toward the lake. Then he rose slowly and headed inside the house. In the hallway, guests were arriving to the party, and he avoided them and left through the side door, car keys in hand.

Strung to the eaves of the garage was a colorful paper banner: "Welcome Back!" Vedran stretched up and ripped the banner down, balling the thin paper in his hands. He climbed into the car and stuffed the wad into the glove box, next to a small brown package. After three turns of the ignition, the Yugo jolted to life, the engine emitting a metallic whine. Vedran had fixed the electrical circuit multiple times before, and he had replaced the transmission, all four tires, the AM radio, even the wipers. His wife treated the car like a family heirloom and wanted it someday to be a gift for their grown daughter. Marta wouldn't want it, he knew that. He was glad, at least, the Yugo allowed him to escape the house.

Vedran sped the car down the drive, whiffing gravel into the air. He downshifted as he approached the gate. Near the lake stood a red deer, its glossy coat the color of rust. The stag raised its head, displaying a magnificent crown of antlers. Vedran pulled over. Instantly he pictured the stag's head as a trophy on his living-room wall. Between the heads of a wild boar and a mouflon, the red deer would be his prized kill. Hart stags were rare in the area and out of season. Surprised by his good fortune, he considered heading back to the house for his rifle, but he would have to contend with his wife and the guests. And then there was Jakov. Vedran reluctantly turned onto the road, hoping the stag would still be around when he came back from town.

The road cut through the forest. On either side chestnut, beech, and hornbeam formed a vast green canopy. Above him a skein of geese glided through the air, soon disappearing from his view. When the trees thinned, he could see a sliver of the lake gleaming in the sunlight. The slate-blue water was a clear kilometer across and shaped like a kidney bean. Years ago, he had taught his daughter to swim in the shallows, and now when she visited home from her university, they still hiked the perimeter together. But after their last argument, he was unsure how long it would be until she returned. His wife cared more about the situation than he did. He preferred to be left alone. Decades ago, he had stumbled into marriage and domestic life. Joining the Croatian Army had been a reprieve, but then he had been injured by shrapnel, and he was discharged, no longer called upon to fight. He came home to find his wife pregnant, and he a father. These days he could barely remember what it felt like to be free of his family.

The train station was in the center of town. A series of flat concrete pillars protruded from its brick façade. Vedran parked in the drop-off bay and kept the engine running, hoping to spot Jakov without having to leave the comfort of the car. While he waited, a steady stream of men and women with children exited through the large glass doors. None of the men resembled the pictures Vedran had seen of Jakov at past gatherings. Jakov was a mystery: an aloof but wealthy man in his wife's family. At Christmas dinner or a relative's birthday, talk invariably centered on Jakov's profitable ventures in South America. Vedran's wife would read aloud Jakov's letters, which bragged of his travels and his stocks and shares, and his lucrative land deals and deep-vein silver mines. After Vedran drunkenly speculated that Jakov was a conman, his wife sent Jakov a great sum of money for a long-term investment.

Vedran tapped the clock on the dashboard and compared the time to his wristwatch. He was late. He got out of the car and checked for traffic police. Seeing none, he bolted up the steps to the entrance and peered through the grimy glass. Smudged figures circulated on the other side, heading to the platforms or the station café. He opened the door and rushed to the arrivals board, where he studied the times. Jakov's train had arrived thirty minutes ago. Vedran scoured the platform but found no sign of Jakov. He asked the conductor if he had seen a lost man, and then he checked at the ticket office. Many men get off at the wrong stop, the clerk told him.

Vedran dismissed the clerk's suggestion. Jakov wouldn't have made such a mistake—he was a world traveler. Vedran tramped back into the foyer and entered the café. Inside, a young barista cleaned the espresso machine behind the counter. Old men were seated nearby, flipping through newspapers and smoking. Vedran studied the men's faces, attempting to recollect Jakov's features: only his bulbous nose came to mind. One man wearing a dingy brown suit fit Vedran's hazy mental image, and he was sitting in the corner, a tan leather suitcase by his feet. The man's face was sunburned and creased, his skin dry as hide. Vedran was surprised at Jakov's poor condition—he had always been under the impression they were roughly the same age. Life in South America had clearly taken its toll.

On the table sat a beat-up fedora, its band missing. Jakov was hunched over his hat, puffing greedily on a cigarillo.

"My wife told you to meet me outside," said Vedran. "I've been waiting."

Jakov jabbed his cigarillo at the demitasse cup in front of him. "It's been a long time since I've enjoyed a good espresso."

"My wife can make you one at the house."

"Ah, yes, Anamarija," said Jakov. "Are you the husband?"

"Yes."

Jakov exchanged his cigarillo for the cup. "I've heard a lot about you. And young Marta."

"We can talk in the car. I left it running."

"Do you still have the family's old 55?"

"Yes, come on. I'll show you."

Jakov waved for Vedran to sit, then sipped his espresso.

Vedran picked up Jakov's suitcase. "There's no time."

Jakov puffed on his cigarillo once more and then extinguished it in his cup.

At the car, Vedran stowed the suitcase in the trunk. Stuck to the topside were worn labels written in exotic languages, which to Vedran made sense only by the image of a palm tree or the word *Hotel*. He knew from his wife that Jakov had been traveling for two days: airplanes to Paris, then Zagreb, a final train out to the countryside.

As Jakov hobbled over, Vedran opened the passenger-side door and gestured for Jakov to sit. Jakov removed his fedora and fanned his face. Tufts of fluffy white hair ringed a shiny bald scalp. "Wait," he said. "I had something else in the baggage car."

Vedran glanced at his wristwatch, then at Jakov. He could smell on him tobacco and an awful cologne, which almost hid the faint scent of whisky.

"I must be getting old," said Jakov. "I'll be one minute."

Vedran felt exasperated as Jakov hurried back to the station. Vedran slammed the door shut and went around the other side of the car. He sat behind the wheel and dug his rough nails into the faux leather of the seat cover. The vinyl fabric crinkled. It felt brittle—time for him to replace once again. He released his grip, telling himself not to get too worked up. They would be home soon, and Jakov would be his wife's problem. All the guests could go ahead and celebrate this arbitrary passing of time: Jakov's return to Croatia. But not Vedran. He considered the party to be sentimental nonsense. And he had better things to do. Even now, he didn't want to wait around for Jakov and his forgotten baggage—the man was old, scatterbrained. Nothing like Vedran.

Vedran adjusted the rearview mirror. His hair was still a shiny black wave and his mustache thick and coarse. There were lines beneath his eyes, but he felt young. His muscles were firm and ropy, as strong as they had been in the Army. Though he was pushing fifty, he could still fight. His war injury had not slowed him down. When he returned home, he would fetch his hunting rifle and fire a shot into the stag's shoulder blade, right into the nest of nerves and tendons. The deer would die instantly.

As Vedran refocused on the station entrance, a knock came on the window. It was a policeman. He circled his finger in the air. Vedran nodded and released the handbrake. He wove through the parking lot until he saw Jakov emerge through the glass doors, clutching a birdcage covered with a bright red cloth. He drove up to the base of the steps. Jakov climbed in, jostling to get the birdcage on his lap.

"What's in there?"

"A monk parakeet."

"All birds go in the back."

"She stays with me."

"Put it in the back."

"She's in a sour mood from being in the baggage car."

"Fine," said Vedran. "Just make sure it doesn't bother me."

Zipping out of town, Vedran thought of his wife back at the house. She put up with his hunting and his women. They had never spoken about his infidelities until the last one, when his daughter had discovered his affair, his rutting in the forest. Marta had screamed and driven back that very afternoon to her university, where she was studying to become a lawyer. Neither Marta nor his wife understood his point of view. Men needed a variety of women: this was a fact of nature. In truth, his mistress, a sprightly redhead, had shades of the woman he had slept with during the war. He often wondered what had happened to her, where she was in the country. At times, he felt he might still be in love with her.

Jakov poked Vedran's arm. "Daydreamer," he said, "let's

stop here."

Ahead was a cinder-block gas station with a single pump on the concrete forecourt.

"Why?" said Vedran. "There's half a tank."

"I need a smoke. I'm all out."

"Check the glove box," said Vedran. As Jakov stretched his arm around the birdcage, Vedran remembered the balled-up banner celebrating Jakov's return. "No, wait!" he said. "I smoked it." He pulled the car into the gas station, next to the store.

Jakov climbed out but then placed the birdcage on the seat. "If she causes any trouble, sing to her."

"What?"

"Singing soothes her." He eased the door shut and ambled toward the pay window.

Vedran wound the window down and called after Jakov, "What if it goes crazy?"

"Her name is Esmeralda."

"How do you know singing works?"

"The previous owner told me."

Vedran couldn't imagine who had owned the bird before. Perhaps an opera singer or a lover of karaoke. Another eccentric, he knew that. Seeing that Jakov was taking his time with the attendant, Vedran lifted the red cloth and immediately saw a black eye staring back. The parakeet was the size of his fist, its scaly feet clutching the perch. She remained still. Her face and breast were gray. The tiny feathers from the top of her head to her long tail were bright green. In the cage were food and water cups and a circular mirror. He tapped on the bars before sticking his finger inside, wiggling it up and down. Esmerelda fluffed her wings, then fluttered around the cage, landing on the base, where she waddled to the far side. Vedran flipped on the radio to find some music. A rock song blasted from the speakers—a lone guitar wailing. Esmerelda beat her wings, flew up to her perch, and pecked at her mirror. He switched off the radio. "I'm not singing," he said.

When Jakov came back, he settled into his seat and smoothed the sides of the red cloth. "She doesn't like it when I smoke."

"What does she say?"

"Nothing. She gives me a look," said Jakov. "She can't speak, or even squawk."

"It must be the only mute parakeet in the world."

"That's why I bought her. Because she's different."

"And because she likes to hear singing."

"Exactly," said Jakov. "You're catching on."

The tires squealed as Vedran peeled the Yugo out of the parking lot. Jakov plucked a cigarette from the pack and broke off the filter. He smoked in silence. Vedran was glad of the break from Jakov's peculiar behavior. He didn't appear wealthy, but then Vedran knew rich people were often misers.

In the distance, he could see the hills close to his house and the clouds massed above. Against the brilliant blue the white flecks of vapor stilled, resembling the watercolors his wife liked to paint on Sundays. Her pictures hung on almost all the walls of the house—only the main wall of the living room was available for his prized taxidermy and display of antique guns. The battleground, he often joked to his friends.

"Is that a restaurant up ahead?" asked Jakov.

"The owners like to think so."

"I'm hungry. The train had nothing to eat."

"My wife will cook a good dinner."

"I remember her food," said Jakov. "It was awful."

Vedran couldn't disagree, but he didn't want to stop. He drove past the restaurant.

Jakov grabbed Vedran's wrist. "I'll pay."

"I'm going to level with you, Jakov," said Vedran. "Back at the house, there's a party in your honor. A surprise party."

Jakov straightened his posture and let go of Vedran's wrist. "Tell me about it."

"It's my wife's doing. All your relatives are there."

"I doubt they remember me."

"They know you from your letters. My wife likes to read them aloud at every family gathering."

Jakov breathed out a steady column of gray smoke, then ashed his cigarette. "She was always kind, even when she was pregnant. I never met Marta, did I?"

"No," said Vedran. "And you won't. She's away."

"Why? Where is she?"

Vedran pumped the brake pedal, stopping the car in the middle of the road. "Quit the questions," he said, "and we'll get something light."

Only a farm truck sat in front of the restaurant. Vedran parked next to the entrance and hustled Jakov and his birdcage inside. The walls of the dining room were painted aquamarine, while the tablecloths and tasseled shades of the table lamps broadcasted 1970s burnt maroon. They sat in a booth that had a view of the forest. Jakov positioned the birdcage close to the window and raised the cloth so Esmerelda could look out. The sun was low in the sky; russet light streaked through the breaks in the gray cloudbank. From somewhere in the dining room, Vedran heard the muffled voice of a woman, and he saw a round face peering through the porthole window of the kitchen door. When the waitress finally came over for their order, she gave the birdcage a funny look. She was a short, thick-set woman, her head too small for her body. Without looking at a menu, Jakov ordered a cornucopia of traditional dishes. Vedran simply asked for a glass of water. The waitress's glum expression remained unaltered. She waddled off back to the kitchen, barking the order at the chef.

The fact Jakov was his wife's cousin weighed on Vedran. If he upset Jakov, he might unsettle his tenuous relationship with his wife. And he sought to carry on with other women in the future. He would just have to bear the man for now. "You should save some room," said Vedran. "My wife has baked a special cake." He tapped his wristwatch. "And she expected us back by now."

"We'll turn the tables and surprise her by being late."

"Lateness adds to my troubles," said Vedran. "Let's forget about the food. I have some business to take care of."

"Now you're talking my language. What is it?"

"We're both men of the world," said Vedran, leaning over. "In South America, you must have seen some wild animals."

"Sloths, one or two marmosets."

"How about big game?"

"There were wild cats: pumas, jaguars, ocelots. But I never saw any outside of the zoo."

"Well, this is your chance to see a rare beast. There's a red deer by the lake. A hart stag." Vedran arched back, resting his hands on his chest. "So, what do you say to some hunting?"

"I'm too old," Jakov confessed. "A lifetime of work has taken the bloodlust out of me."

"Not me."

"What line of work are you in?"

"I hunt."

"But before?"

"Army," said Vedran, playfully thumping his heart, "then a mechanic."

"And now?"

"Now I do what I want."

"Yes," said Jakov, "you are a man of the world."

Before long the waitress brought over a tray of dishes. A basket of bread already sat on the table, and to this she added a carafe of ice water, a bowl of slimy cottage cheese, and a kulen sausage. The kulen rested on a wooden board along with a serrated knife. The waitress explained they were out of the other food they had ordered and marched off. Jakov laughed at her rudeness, then cut several slices of the smoked pork sausage and chose the end piece to chop into quarters, then eighths, finally spearing one morsel with his fork and feeding it to Esmerelda.

They watched Esmerelda swallow the bit of sausage. Vedran lost his appetite, and any sense of polite eating, when Jakov spooned cottage cheese onto the top of a bread roll and took a sloppy bite. He spoke while chewing his food. Vedran couldn't register what Jakov was saying. Instead he considered whether Jakov knew of his own rudeness, and whether they all had bad eating habits in South America.

"Do parakeets eat meat?"

"Once in a while I like to give her a taste," replied Jakov. "Make her feel like a hawk." He speared another lump of kulen and poked it through the bars of the cage. Esmerelda clutched the scrap in her foot, holding the meat up to her beak so she could rip it apart.

As Jakov continued to feed Esmerelda, the waitress came over. Her small face had reddened, and her breath stank of wine and cigarettes. Tiny patches of burgundy speckled the front of her apron. She looked back and forth between Jakov and Vedran, her finger pointing at the birdcage. "This is a five-star restaurant!" she yelled. "Not a petting zoo."

"Five-star?" Vedran laughed.

"What's funny?" she said. "Get out! Get out!"

Vedran rose from the table and pulled out his wallet. He peeled off a few bills and pressed them into her hand. "Let's go, Jakov."

Jakov waved him down and smiled at the waitress. "Would you like to hold her?"

"Birds belong in the sky."

"Not Esmerelda. She loves people." He opened the cage door and stuck his hand inside. He whispered a few words, and Esmerelda darted onto his palm.

The waitress folded her arms. "Take that thing outside."

He drew Esmerelda close to his face and kissed her beak. "She won't hurt you," he said. "Now, what's your name?"

"Dunja."

Jakov slid out of the booth and stood next to the waitress. "Dunja, show me your hand." When she didn't reply, he took her hand and turned it palm up. Esmerelda hopped over. "There you go," he said.

A few minutes later, in the Yugo, Vedran watched Jakov kiss Dunja and then strut over to the car. He felt tired from dealing with this man. He dug underneath his seat and extricated his bottle of rakija. He glugged a mouthful of the plum brandy, then another, and another, until the dream-like feeling that he was young again washed over him once more.

Jakov leaned inside the car and placed the birdcage on the seat.

"You really charmed her," said Vedran.

"I felt out of practice."

"Nonsense. Women love you. Dunja does." Vedran offered the bottle to Jakov, but he refused.

"I'd like to drive the rest of the way," said Jakov. "It's been years since I've driven this car."

"Where's your bird going to sit?"

"Esmerelda likes you."

Vedran let out a disbelieving grunt. No one liked him. Not his mistress or his wife. Sometimes, he thought, Marta didn't care for him. She loved him, he knew that. But he was not easy to get along with. Hunting was his refuge from thinking about these things. If they hurried back to the house, the stag could still be feeding near the lake. "Fine," he said. "Just drive fast."

The car lurched as Jakov drove. He hunched over the wheel, his eyes fixed on the verdant land. He talked about the beauty of the area and how he had missed the hills and forests. He couldn't believe, he said, when he had left Yugoslavia that he would return to a fractured republic.

"I fought for our independence," said Vedran. "What did you do?"

"I've never been interested in politics."

Vedran lifted the bottle over the top of the cage and took another slug of the rakija. "You left the country. You didn't have to deal with Milošević."

"I had my own problems to deal with," said Jakov. "South America has its share of crazed strongmen."

"I want to know what you did for Hrvatska."

"Why do you care?"

"You skipped out when the war began."

"My business over there helped people back here."

"I doubt that."

"You can't let the war go. Forget about it. Enjoy your hunting instead."

"I do. I've earned my retirement."

"That you have," replied Jakov. "And I'd say to you, my brother, that I have the country in my heart, that the beauty of the land and women around us and the freedom we have is a testament to the sacrifices of patriots, men such as yourself."

Vedran raised the bottle. "Živjeli," he said. As soon as he finished his sip of brandy, he felt foolish and doubtful of the sincerity of Jakov's little speech. Jakov's smug grin curdled Vedran's resolve not to upset his wife's cousin. Jakov had no right in chastising him for the pleasures he enjoyed in his retirement, or in invoking his military service. Unlike the waitress, he wouldn't fall for Jakov's charisma. As Vedran considered a rebuttal to Jakov's hollow rhetoric, the car veered onto a gravel road and accelerated. Shudders vibrated through the cab. Vedran clutched the bars of the birdcage so that it wouldn't slip from his lap.

"You took a wrong turn," said Vedran.

"There's something I want to see."

"Turn us around." Vedran glanced out the window. "Why don't you listen to anything I say?"

"This won't take long."

"My wife is expecting you."

"I haven't seen her in twenty years," said Jakov. "She can wait a moment longer."

Jakov drove up the road, winding through the dense forest. On one side the trees winnowed away, the glittering waters of the lake peeking through gaps in the foliage. Jakov parked the car on the berm and blinked the headlights, illuminating a dirt path. Complaining that his back ached, Jakov demanded Vedran carry Esmerelda. Vedran considered arguing with Jakov, but so far it had gotten him nowhere. "Whatever you want to see," he said. "Let's be quick."

They hopped a low fence and hiked through a grove of beech trees to a clearing of ryegrass. In front of them stood the lakeshore. The sun was dipping below the hills, the sky now brimming with brilliant oranges and reds. On the far side of the lake was the family house. A column of black smoke curled out of the chimney. Vedran thought he could hear the distant echo of a stag belling. The stag, he presumed, warning off a rival hart.

"Your wife and I used to watch sunsets from this spot," said Jakov. "Once, just after the war started, we saw MiG jets fly over the house."

Vedran set the birdcage on a flat rock. "She never told me that."

"It was so long ago." Jakov bent over the birdcage and slowly pulled off the cloth. "I invited her to Rio, but she had other matters to attend to."

The news stumped Vedran. His wife had never mentioned

this possible trip to South America.

"Esmeralda feels at home here," said Jakov. "Look how relaxed she is. She loves the forest, the water. She'll be a perfect gift for Marta."

"There's no room for you or your bird at the house," said Vedran. "Marta's room is off-limits. She'll be back in a few days."

"It will be good to finally meet her," he said.

"She's strong-willed," said Vedran, "and stubborn, like my wife."

"I'm sure neither of them will mind me staying."

"How about a hotel? You're rich. You can spare it."

"My assets are tied up in a land deal."

"Even the money my wife gave you?"

"Yes, it's all invested in rainforest." Jakov appeared to sense Vedran's incredulity, and he carried on with a long-winded explanation of Brazilian zoning laws and the permits needed for a hydroelectric dam. "The government will be on board very soon."

"Sure, I get it. So, why are you back?"

"To see my family," said Jakov.

"Not because you're broke."

"That's silly. I love my cousin, all my relatives."

Vedran doubted Jakov's wish to see the rest of the family. Jakov was a conman—Vedran had been right about that. Vedran stooped down to eye Esmerelda. Freshly molted feathers lay on the cage floor. A tiny bald patch marked her chest. He knew birds occasionally pecked out their feathers when they felt distressed or spent long periods in captivity. He unlocked the door and reached in for Esmerelda. She dodged his grasp and flew onto the frame of the mirror.

Vedran whispered the first verse of an old lullaby—one that he had used to soothe Marta when she was young. Only a week before, in a moment of unexpected sentimentality, he had recorded the song and mailed the tape to her. A day later, the package returned unopened. His wife said he should quit drinking and quit womanizing and go to see his daughter, apologize in person. For appearances he had ruminated on a visit, but he wasted most of the week drinking and mulling over a call to his mistress.

Esmerelda flitted to her perch. Vedran didn't think he had gotten the melody quite right, but she still scampered onto his hand. She felt light, barely there. He withdrew his arm and held her up so their faces were close. Esmerelda darted to his shoulder. He petted her crown with his fingertip.

"She trusts you," said Jakov. "I trust you."

"When are we going to get our money back?"

Jakov picked up the cage and glanced back toward the car. "It's getting late. You can put her back now."

"There's a half-hour of daylight," said Vedran. "Plenty of time for us to keep talking."

"I've been thinking about the party. Let's go eat some cake and be nice to your wife. I can call Marta and tell her about her new bird." Jakov pointed to the other side of the lake. "And you can hunt the stag."

Across the water, Vedran could see a speck of red. The stag looked less majestic at this distance. Less important. He was starting to come around to his wife's suggestion about Marta. Perhaps he would drive to Zagreb in the morning and check if Marta would take the car. She would call *him* father while having no idea about the presence of her blood relative. Jakov would never be part of her life.

"I'll get the stag later," said Vedran. He brushed Esmerelda off his shoulder. She beat her wings and crested up, just above his head, where he could hear the gentle flutter of her escape. Jakov reached up to coax her down, to allow her to perch on his finger. He hummed a tune, then broke out into the lyrics of a folk song. Vedran circled behind Jakov and clasped his hand over Jakov's mouth. Jakov jolted backward, his fedora becoming crooked on his head. He tried to speak. His spittle wetted Vedran's fingers. "No more singing," said Vedran, "and no more talking about my wife or daughter."

Against the sky Esmerelda's face darkened; her iridescent wings glowed cobalt blue, then a majestic, all-encompassing green. She flew higher, moving over the lake, drifting away on the warm currents. Her flightpath, Vedran conjectured, took her to the hills and the sprawl of forest that stretched to the border. He visualized her route—thinking of the treetop she would soon land in and begin to build a nest—so when his wife asked him: Where is my cousin? Is he excited to see me? No, he could say. For Jakov had decided to go back to South America and leave the family alone.

All The Land Before Us

For the seventh day in a row my father and I settle down in the trench. We are far from the conflict here on the outskirts of Đurđevac, where we own a pig farm. The front line between us Croats and the Serbs sits over a hundred kilometers away. Our region is so inconsequential MiGs haven't bothered to buzz us for months—until yesterday, when they mistakenly shelled a dog pound on the other side of town. Almost forty dogs escaped, and, to while away the time, my father forced me into a competition to see who can shoot the most strays. In a circular span of eighty meters, a half-dozen carcasses lie in the dirt.

When my father climbs the ladder out of the trench, he surveys the carnage of the last day. He is an able marksman, though not good enough to be a sniper and too old to serve in the HV. I have deliberately missed my shots. The dogs remind me of our own—two glossy black sheepdogs—and of my mother stuck at home, looking after them.

Across the field an Alsatian emerges from the woods and sniffs a pile of bloodied sinew and bone. The animal stands erect, the sheen of its tan-and-black coat showing off its size and pedigree. I train the rifle sights on the dog's head, then across to the thick of its neck. My father is over in the hut behind a stand of oak trees, and I hope the dog runs off before he sees it. I am sick of the game, the festering bodies that bloat blue and black in the summer sun.

I lower the rifle and slouch in the pit of the trench. The cool dark soil reminds me of the spring, before my father's bankruptcy and before his obsession began. For half the summer, my father and I dug the eight-meter trench on the far side of our property line. The border with Hungary sits a few kilometers away, and my father is paranoid the Serbs will rout our military by this backdoor. He likes to bring up France's Maginot Line and the Germans sidestepping the fortified defenses through Belgium.

My father returns and stands atop the ladder, his hands clutching a pair of tin cups. Sweat pearls his forehead, slicking the dirt that has temporarily colored his gray hair. He is pushing sixty and is older than my friends' fathers. They are away fighting for our independence.

I squint up at him, annoyed he has come back so quickly. Part of me wishes he was on the front line with those other men. I am done with this heat and this trench and his orders. My father grunts for my help, and I prop the rifle against the side of the trench. He hunches over and hands me the tin cups. Then he shinnies down the rickety steps. "Any luck, Josip?" he says.

"I thought I saw something, but it was a shadow."

He peers over the top of the trench, binoculars pressed to his face, then gestures for his cup. "There's a big one, an Alsatian, sixty meters out."

I drink some gemišt, glad of the excuse not to say anything. Though we have been drinking this watered-down wine for hours, I cannot bear to watch him kill any more dogs. Gaseous odors from the pools of leaked bile have begun to reach the trench. Without the relief of any breeze, the high sun makes it all worse, and my bandanna once soaked with sweat now seems to have absorbed the stink of death.

"You need this one," he says. "To catch up."

I exchange my cup for the rifle and steady the barrel on the lip of the trench. The dog scampers around the field, finally stopping near another carcass. Above the Alsatian, white clouds shift in the wide blue sky. The glassy sound of the stream beyond the barbed-wire fence burns my ears. From where I stand, I sense my father behind me, urging me on. I can smell his strong wine breath and several days of rank sweat. I close my eyes and finger the trigger lightly, surprised by the sudden jolt. A high-pitched yowl forces me to look: dark blood oozes from the Alsatian's hind leg. Instinctively, the dog whips around and whimpers into the woods.

My father slaps the back of my head. "Come on, relieve it of its pain," he says.

"The dog's gone."

"It's hiding," he says. "And suffering."

"We should let nature take its course."

"That's not right." His body hulks over my spindly fifteen-year-old version, suspended between youth and what my father likes to call my impending manhood. He punches my shoulder and gestures to the ladder.

I step around him, unwilling to suffer his hand again.

"Leave the rifle," he says. "Take this." He draws the Luger from his holster and presses it into my palm. The burnish on the blued finish seems darker than I remember. The pistol is my grandfather's, who boasted of its killing efficiency during the Second World War. He was a member of the fascist Ustaše movement and regretted little in his dealings with the Serbs.

Out of the trench, I trudge past what looks to be a mongrel boxer, blackflies covering its eye sockets and large pink tongue lolling from the side of its mouth. I pass more carcasses, unable to discern the breeds. All I can see are stiff limbs, folded over, jutting into the air. Strings of intestines decompose nearby in the grass.

I slip my bandanna down to cover my nose and mouth. I keep walking, now at a faster pace. Crows linger near the remains and hawks fly overhead. All of them have been feasting. I look away, somewhat relieved, the buzz from the gemišt vanquished. A trail of bloodspots leads into the trees, and I glance back to the trench. There is no sign of my father. I push on, thankful for the absence of his watchful eye. In the dense underbrush I stumble over knots of fallen limbs and lose track of the blood. I rest against a tree and listen for the Alsatian. Jangles from a dog tag crest the air, and I follow the sound the best I can, weaving a path through endless oak and beech, soon losing my way from the familiar side of the woods. I debate whether to fire a shot into the air and then backtrack. I can tell my father that the dog is dead and I am going home to see my mother. But a suffocating pressure within me says I should keep going, and I start toward the blades of sunlight up ahead.

A logging road breaks the swath of trees. I look each way, trying to get my bearings. Just down the road a sign points the way to the Drava River, the natural border with Hungary, and beyond to the scattered farmhouses starring the horizon. From this distance the little white blocks resemble the buildings here. The people I imagine are much the same: born of the farms and flatlands and the web of streams and rivers that crisscross this entire region. Heavy rains can engulf the floodplains, my mother often reminds me, and vast slivers of land disappear every summer.

I hurry along the side of the road, unsure of where exactly

I am. I finger the safety of the Luger. After a short while, I hear an engine straining to come up the road. I stick the pistol in my waistband and cover it with my shirt. I wave as the car approaches, slows in a ball of dust. It is a boxy Skoda, the color of dry mud. A woman sticks her hand out the window. She looks to be older, in her twenties. She has short greasy black hair, cut irregularly, and wears a plain T-shirt and blue jeans. I smile but I don't recognize her. She probably lives in one of the other towns not far from here.

The woman trundles her car alongside me, and I pull the bandanna down to my neck. "Can I get a ride?"

"Where are you going?"

"Home," I say, "but I'm lost."

She pulls over. I go around to the passenger's side and open the door. In an awkward series of maneuvers, she manages to heave her large duffel bag to the backseat. She appears embarrassed at the collection of socks and underwear strewn about. Tangled bras hang over a stack of thick books.

"Look forward," she says, then tells me her name is Luna.

"Josip," I say.

She drives for a while before speaking again. As she asks about the town of Nova Rača, I realize her accent is off, that she is Hungarian. I have never heard of the town—and I feel my face indicating the same thought. "My sister lives there," she continues. "I thought it was nearby, but I don't know this area very well."

"That makes two of us."

"You said you were from around here."

"I am, but over there." I point at the woods. The line of trees runs alongside the road all the way to the horizon.

Luna shakes her hair with her eyes closed, and the car

weaves into the middle of the road. Her face looks soft, slightly sunburned. I like the way she looks, the fact that she seems untroubled by the world. She steers back into the correct lane. "There's a map next to you. Try to find out where we are."

I take the map from the door pocket and unfold it on my lap. I trace my finger over the topographic markers, the large blocks of green and tan. The region is all farms and small towns and woods and flat fields. The writing is in Magyar, and I cannot find a landmark I recognize.

"You wouldn't be much use in this war."

"I look after my mother. She needs me." I say this as I know I should shield my mother from my father. She stays at home with the sheepdogs, putting up with my father's drunkenness, his shouting, his open-fist slaps. When I am in the house, I hear the chorus of barks echo through the walls to my room, where I lie in bed, paralyzed.

"You're a good boy."

I sit up in the seat, extend my legs out in a show. I am taller than she is. "I'm eighteen."

She laughs. "I know," she says. "I was married at that age."

I join in with her laughter, unsure if she knows I am lying. I wish I had some gemišt with me; I could prove to her that I am a man. I check the rearview mirror to see if there is any alcohol on the backseat. A jumble of unopened letters and rolls of gauze and opaque pill bottles lies to the side of her duffel bag. I sense she is not telling me something, that her sister is not expecting her. I fold the map and stash it away. "You have a smoke?"

She nods to the center console and asks if I would light one for her. I stick two cigarettes between my lips, ignite the

ends, and breathe in. I feel a rush of smoke in my lungs—
even when I pass over a cigarette and exhale, my chest
remains heavy. I haven't smoked for months. The day my
father learned he would have to sell our pigs, he beat the
habit out of me, then slaughtered all the sows. Later, my
torso blacked with bruises, he came to my room and
mumbled something about my lack of hard work and how
it was my mother's fault.

Smoke swirls around the cab, and Luna and I crank
our windows. As she rotates the handle, the curve of her
breasts presses against her T-shirt. Her nipples poke against
the fabric, and I realize she is not wearing a bra. She drives
one-handed, whispering under her breath, occasionally
flicking ash into the warm air. As she finishes her cigarette,
she confesses that she has left her husband. I assure her
that is good, but she does not acknowledge what I have
said. Instead she begins a story about her life before she
got married. She attended Mass every week but wished the
church would burn down with everyone trapped inside
it. "I wanted to be erased," she says. "Incinerated beyond
recognition. Then I met Tamás and we married and moved
away, and I forgot all about that feeling."

She glances at me to see what I think of her. I have
never been with a woman, but I feel it is right to touch
her hand and squeeze the underside. She lets our fingers
stay intertwined. Even when she has to scratch an itch on
the side of her face, she draws our hands up together to
her cheek. Perhaps something more will happen before we
reach her sister's. Perhaps I will stay with her. I can call my
mother later.

The road forks, and Luna veers to the right without

asking me. She seems steeped in her own silence, in thinking about the path of her life. I want her to tell me more about Tamás and why she left him. As I ask her about her husband, we both spot something sprawled on the road ahead. Luna slams her foot to the brake pedal, and I lose her hand to the steering wheel. At the same time we both now see it is an animal, curled up, a stocky crescent of hair. I presume she is going to drive around it, but she switches off the engine.

"What are you doing?" I ask.

"Helping."

"It's roadkill."

"No look, it's a dog."

"We should carry on to your sister's. I think it's back the other way."

"I have to see if I can save it."

She hurries out of the car and approaches the dog without a care. From this distance, the animal could be a host of different breeds, another dog from the pound. I roll the window back up, hoping this will all go away. Then I hear Luna call out. I exit the car slowly. My walk over wants to turn into a run into the trees. As I get close, I recognize the pained face of the Alsatian. Shallow breaths come from its mouth, and its wet eyes lock with mine. The dog's legs are twisted and soaked with blood. Luna kneels next to it. I worry she will be able to tell that the dog has been shot, that I am the perpetrator. But she says the dog must have been hit by a car.

I stand behind her, looking at the road. "It's lost a lot of blood."

"Do you know any vets around here?"

"No," I say. "We should leave it alone."

"He's someone's pet."

"More likely a guard dog. One that's run away."

"I didn't think you'd be so uncaring." She reaches out to stroke the dog's head and it snaps at her. She tries again, whispering that he is a good boy, but this time it nips her finger and she recoils. She sucks on her finger, and when she draws it out of her mouth, I notice a tooth has punctured her skin.

Luna heads back to the car and I follow, sensing this is the end of the matter. She clambers into the backseat and roots through her duffel bag and brings out a pair of stockings. Then she turns back to the dog.

"You hold its jaw closed," she says.

I kneel to the side of its head and launch my hands around its snout. The animal widens its jaws against my clasped hands. Globs of warm spittle wet my fingertips. Luna loops the stockings around the Alsatian's muzzle and ties a knot. "Pick him up," she says. "Gently."

I scoop up the dog and pull its weight into my chest. I can feel a groove in its thigh, and I caress the edge of the wound. Damp spreads through my shirtfront. Luna runs ahead of me and clears a space on the backseat. I lean in and lay the dog on its side. Urine stains the outside of my clothes.

Luna doesn't notice or care. She starts the engine and stamps on the accelerator. "Where can we take him?"

"There are pig farms around here, but I'm unsure what good a farmer can do."

"They have bandages, medicines," she says. "We can save him."

As she drives, I glance back now and again. A low-pitched whine emerges from the back of the dog's throat. Its chest rises and falls. Luna jerks the car to a halt in front of a cottage. She sizes up the darkened windows. She blares the horn. When no one comes out, she says, "What's wrong with people?" I rub her arm and volunteer to get help. She tells me to be quick.

Nobody answers my knock on the door, so I peer through the bay window at the front of the house. All the furniture has been removed, and the carpets ripped up, leaving the floorboards exposed. Above the fireplace, squares of bluish-white shade the wall. Any pictures of who lived here are long gone. I walk around to the back and sit on the wood steps. A pigpen sits abandoned at the end of the overgrown lawn. I venture over, see the puddles and wet mud, a few strands of straw and rotten apples in the slop trough. Trotter prints reveal a path to a corrugated iron hutch. Beyond, the enclosure fields appear as a patchwork of gray now that the sky is darkening. As I lean against the fence, feeling the spit of rain against my face, I wonder how long Luna will wait for me.

When I return, the Skoda is idling and the headlamps are on. The dark shape of her body appears static, but I imagine her in the river with me, the two of us splashing around, then standing together, soaked, our hipbones pushing together.

The door is locked, so I tap the window. Luna's cutting her hair even shorter. She leans over and holds the scissors close to the window. A lock of dark hair appears caught in the sharp blades. She blows the lock toward me—a few hairs stick to the glass, revealing her blonde roots. She drops the scissors in the center console and unlocks the door. I sit next to her, slightly troubled, and I explain that the cottage is empty, that the people must have left when war broke out.

Without replying, she starts off again. She speeds up to seventy. Then faster. The speedometer hovers near ninety. Rain pelts against the windshield, the wipers achieving little in the downpour. The bumps in the road vibrate through the chassis. Beams of light illuminate a half dozen meters of gravel in front of us. It is hard to tell where we are now.

A ghoulish whine fills the car. The dog's ragged breath becomes weak and erratic, worsened by the tight knot of the stockings. "It's dying," I say. "We shouldn't let it suffer."

Her foot eases off the pedal and she lets the Skoda drift down the road. "I don't know what to do."

I raise my shirt. She sees the pistol. I expect her to be surprised, but she seems relieved and pulls the car over. She looks at my bare waist, the whiteness outlining the solid hunk of black steel. She stretches out her hand, but I drop my shirt, afraid if she handles the pistol she will realize I shot the dog.

"I'll do it," I say.

We go around to the back of the car. Storm clouds fill the sky all the way to the horizon. Waves of gray lash down and rake the tree line. I look away from the woods to the dog's limp body. I lift the Alsatian and cradle its head, sheltering its eyes from the rain. I want to say something to Luna about my mother and father, about the war, about the land and the rivers, about the two of us, but the words don't come.

"After it's done, we'll go back to that cottage," she says, "and warm ourselves with a fire."

She reaches for my shoulder, but I have already stepped away. The Alsatian's thick coat is soaked heavily with sweat and urine and blood, and raindrops glide off its matted hair.

The dog writhes helplessly, then falls still as I hike into the woods. Once I am clear of Luna's view, I kneel next to a tall oak tree and roll the dog onto its side. I untie the stockings and stuff them into my pocket. I want the dog to breathe, to enjoy one more gulp of air. I stand and draw the pistol, aim at the dog's head. A film glosses its brown eyes, and its body shivers, rhythmically, settling down to an almost imperceptible movement. Ghostly aches run through me, from inside my bones out to the contours of my body. Before I can stop myself, I raise my arm and fire into the tree trunk—the bullet lodging deep in the heartwood. I know Luna, my father, all the men in the war would have killed the dog.

Above the noise of the rainstorm, I hear Luna shout my name. I duck as low as I can and watch her. She holds a book above her head, her eyes squinting. She steps into the woods and calls for me once again. Though she cannot see me, she asks if everything is alright. I slip around to the other side of the oak. I flatten my back against the bark, close my eyes, and pray for her to leave.

After a while, I look back. She is still there, smoking in the rain. Her T-shirt is slick against her body. She stares in my direction and flicks her cigarette into the woods. Then she disappears from my view. When I hear the car speed away, I check on the dog. I study the light in its eyes for a moment and then press Luna's stockings to my nose. Everywhere around me it is gray, and I imbibe more dog than woman. I stick the stockings back into my pocket and kneel in the dirt. I touch the animal's soft underbelly, and run my fingers up to its chest, feeling the lungs inflate, then collapse. After the last thrum of the dog's heart, I drop the pistol and head in the rough direction of home, hoping I can find my way back. I grope through the darkness of the woods for hours. I wonder if my mother has escaped my father's drunken behavior tonight. Sometimes she is more scared of him than I am. Perhaps I should have saved the Luger. She could have ended his tyranny for us both.

This thought stays with me as I break from the trees. The rain has eased off and left a glittering sheen on the fields. I struggle over the barbed-wire fence. In the distance, a kilometer or so over the ridge, lies the house. Closer to my position stands the hut, a yolk of orange from the kerosene lamp haloes in the window.

I walk toward the light. My father is going to be angry at me, even violent, when he learns I lost his pistol. Years from now, after I have left this place, I know I will return home—the war long over—and I imagine us celebrating the new millennium. I would leave my girlfriend in Zagreb to come to my father's party, just him and a few of his friends. My mother is gone, and he pretends not to remember her name. Her sheepdogs, now gray and arthritic, live muted in the pigpen. On the first day of the new year, the land blanketed with snow, he has me search the woods for the Luger, retracing my steps. He follows me into the thick of the trees, but I run off through the snow. My memory guides me to where the dog died, yards from where I last saw Luna. I brush away snow from the ground in front of the oak. I dig through dirt and bone, cleave the earth for the pistol, finally ready to confront my father.

That time is not now. The lamplight flickers, and I step on something soft and wet, my footing unsteady, gone, sending me twisted into the grass. Around me, strewn across this waterlogged land, lies misshapen chunks of dog flesh and internal organs. Farther away sit furred limbs and crooked heads, muzzles pointing to the sky. I kick a ribcage away. I rise to my feet and stagger across the field, my eyes fixed on the dimming light. I reach the outside of the hut as the kerosene burns out, and I listen for my father. I cannot hear anything, but I fear he is inside. I stumble around in the wideness of the inky night, looking for the trench, blind to its location until my boot hits the ladder rail. I climb down the steps, wondering if my father is here. I whisper for him. I call out for my father. There is no reply. I lie down, unwilling to stand anymore. My face presses into the wet dirt; I breathe in the earth and wait for the rain to start up again.

The Little Girls

The morning after his daughter's death, Mislav stumbles out of his cottage carrying her dolls and feeling their weight in his hands growing heavier with every step. He lays the dolls on the lawn to catch the sun. As the heat rises, he sits in the grass and watches the sun light up their faces. He wishes his wife were here to drive him to the morgue. He can hardly stay awake, yet he keeps watch on the road, the single artery of asphalt that leads into town. He cannot hear the thrum of his wife's car or the radio she loves to play so loud. His daughter disliked music, pop or otherwise. She preferred silence. She would have appreciated this moment. They would have enjoyed it together.

Bright sunlight stirs Mislav in the early afternoon. He squints at the empty driveway. Before the war, his wife always informed him of her whereabouts. Then he was called up to serve in the HV. While he was away, often for months at a time, he sensed from her letters that she was glad he was rarely around. When the war ended, she told him they would remain together purely for the sake of their daughter.

He rises from the soft grass and takes the dolls to his workshop, where he clamps the tallest doll into the vise and presses a hacksaw against its lower torso. He strokes the hacksaw back and forth, a slow cut, legs tumbling to the floor. He cleans flecks of pinkish vinyl from the blade, then selects the next doll. As he saws off the legs, he speaks his young daughter's name *Kata*, over and over, until the name becomes a primeval sound, two raw syllables, nothing else.

She was small, undersized for her age. She had turned eleven not long ago and suffered from cystic nodule acne. Recently, she had stolen her mother's makeup and astringent creams. He had talked with Kata about her blemishes, reassuring her that she was as God made her. He encouraged her to forget about her appearance and enjoy playing skrivača and slijepi miš. She chased the neighbor's boys to trip them. She loved the copse of beech trees in the hills.

Mia, Lara, Ines, Natali, Hana.

She had named the trees after her dolls.

Mislav wants to remember his daughter this way, but all he can think of are his neighbor's words, his mention of the landmine, Kata's foot found in a pile of leaves.

When his wife finally returns home, she finds Mislav in Kata's bedroom flipping through one of her storybooks. Mislav glances at his wife. She is wearing her old shearling coat, which he gave her before the war. Her eyes seem cloudy, her lips bright and bruised.

"This was her favorite," he says.

"You're useless," his wife screams. "A useless father." She slaps his chest and the edge of his jaw.

He raises the book to protect his face. "I'm sorry," he says.

"You should have been watching her."

"I know."

"I'll never forgive you."

He lowers the book and searches his wife's face for intent. Her head is bowed, her anger gone, replaced by desperate sadness. He drops the book. Then he holds his wife, his hands knotted around her back. She rests her head on his shoulder. He can smell her day-old perfume and the cigarettes she has smoked, her many glasses of šljivovica, and the sour odor of another man. Where she has been does not matter. He tells himself this, like he has so many times before.

"We should be with Kata," he says.

She squirms inside his hug: her fingers run tenderly under his workshirt, then her nails scratch across his ribs. He releases his grip, concerned she will go on to hurt herself if he refuses. She sits on the edge of the bed, folding her hands in her lap. She looks past Mislav to the wooden toy chest in the corner.

While his wife sleeps in Kata's bed, Mislav slips out to his workshop. He has a hazy idea of memorializing his daughter's life. He assesses the pallet of lumber and chooses a good piece, cutting the hardwood to the length of a child's body. Through the swirling motes of sawdust, he has a vision of the little girls. He hammers five nails through the plank. Then he strips the dolls of their frilly dresses and white cotton undergarments, and he dabs a rag dosed with mineral spirits on their faces to clean away the crayoned red dots. With his fingertip, he smooths their sable hair. Finally, he slides the dolls into the iron nails, puncturing the torsos.

In his vegetable garden, Mislav sets up the little girls, their gazes directed toward the hills and the beech trees. The paint has started to flake around their mouths. He thumbs Ines' lips, wiping off a few salmon-colored fragments. Her serene expression reminds him that when he gave Ines to his daughter, Kata screamed that he had bought the wrong doll.

In the morning, Mislav's wife brings the local newspaper to him in bed. Her hair is up, fastened with a silver barrette, brushed for the first time in days. Hard lines have formed around her eyes, visible now with her face free of makeup. She has refused to speak of the little girls, of her lover, of the death of her daughter. She slumps against the headboard. She spreads out the newspaper and jabs at the headline on the second page—a warning about landmines.

"Was this your fault?" she asks.

"A different unit buried these," he says. "I didn't know about them."

"You should have."

Mislav buried landmines during the war, but far away, close to the border. He tells his wife about wartime defenses, the forgotten landmines scattered across Croatia, but her head and heart seem closed off from his words. She rolls onto the newspaper. She groans, her eyes glazed. She has taken her prescription painkillers again. Mislav straddles his wife and yanks her nightgown up to her waist, exposing the tangle of black pubic hair. She opens her legs mechanically, but he ignores her gesture and crawls to the end of the bed, where he lifts her foot, cupping the arch to inspect the ridges and odd bumps. He kisses her heel, then slides his tongue between her toes, licking the thin crescents of skin. The muscles in her calves and thighs quiver. She complains he is tickling her, and she bucks her leg. But he holds her ankle tight and bites the side of her foot.

"Ne. Prestani!" she says.

"Come to the morgue with me."

"I can't."

"I'll bite you again."

"Mislav, why are you like this?"

"You're my wife. We should go there together."

"It won't make any difference."

Over the next several days neither Mislav nor his wife visits the morgue. Each time she refuses, the bedtime ritual becomes more elaborate: he bites her feet, then washes them with bowls of cistern rainwater and pads her soles dry with squares of soft terrycloth. He cuts her toenails with knife-edge scissors and trims the fine blonde hairs that encircle her moles. Then he rubs in lavender oil, which slicks her bruised skin and colorizes the sickly yellows and blackened purples. When he presses his thumbs into her ligaments and across her bones, she whimpers into the gray of the room.

Before the nightly biting, he counts her toes. "What should we name them?"

After attending the funeral alone, Mislav comes home to find his wife sitting on the toy chest. Her open robe reveals her naked body. He stands his wife up; she sways on her swollen feet. He guides her to their bedroom and leaves a bucket by the nightstand. For hours he drinks in his workshop. At some point in the night, he eyes the jars of creosote and turpentine on the windowsill. His death would be slow: internal burns, convulsions, a fall into unconsciousness. If he believed in Heaven, he would see Kata again. But his lip service toward a belief in God, in the doctrine of Catholicism, was a ruse to appease his daughter. Now he stares at the jar of black oil, imagines the coal-tar liquid sticking to the back of his throat, choking the remaining life from his body. He clutches the jar, presses the cold glass against his chest, and unscrews the lid. Then he hears voices outside—a man whispering to a woman. Shadows flit across the windowpane. A car starts, drives away.

In time, Mislav reluctantly sympathizes with his wife's affair, her new life on the Dalmatian coast. He didn't offer her very much. Yet he knows he has lost something, some large part of his life. He spends his days erecting a wooden fence around the copse of beech trees. He nails warnings to the posts, the whole time eyeing the landmine crater. The trees cast a shadow over the misshapen hole. He strains to forget about his daughter's foot blown into the air and thumping down in a bed of pale brown leaves. Why hadn't one of the neighbor's boys died instead?

When winter storms envelop the land, Mislav abandons his hikes into the hills, afraid of the pearled sky. He drinks glasses of his wife's šljivovica and swishes in painkillers, sometimes sleeping tablets. He stays in the cottage, watching the skiffs of snow blow through the valley and settle into drifts on the hills. He stokes the fire; he slowly burns through his woodpile. Most nights, by firelight, he pores over his daughter's copy of *Croatian Tales of Long Ago*. He read these fairy tales to Kata when she was little, enchanting her with forest goblins and young boys lost in the glade. She asked what the stories meant. He had an answer then, but the stories make no sense to him anymore. Nothing does. So he gorges on kulen and slanina and large bits of curd cheese. He devours knots of sweet bucolaj bread. His legs and belly become fat. His breathing shallows. He despises his wife and the idea of his old neighbor fondling her feet.

Foul odors rouse Mislav in the spring. A dull ache runs through his body as he surveys the yard. Weeds have overgrown the vegetable garden. He tears out every type of plant: sow thistle, black bryony, fennel, refusing to stop until ox tongue spikes his hands. Standing up straight, he notices tomato vines corkscrewed around the bodies of the little girls. He plucks an unripe tomato and swallows it whole. The second he bites, splitting the green flesh in two. After he devours all the fruit, he curls up with the dolls, maneuvering his fat arm around the line of spikes. He drifts off and dreams of his daughter safe in bed.

Stabbing pains wake Mislav late in the afternoon. A nail has grazed his arm. He sits up and smears the blood with the back of his hand. The exposed nail sticks out from Ines— his daughter's favorite. But that was not always so. Ines was the wrong doll, the unwanted toy abandoned behind the dollhouse.

As he slides Ines off the nail, he recalls his daughter's gentle breaths, the small red bumps on her face, the spurt of puberty just beginning to bud. It must have been a year until Kata cradled the doll and proclaimed that she was her best friend. She told Ines versions of her beloved fairy tales. Stories of forests and goblins and sea-maidens. Mislav was glad it had distracted his daughter from the brutality of the war.

Now he carries Ines, and he heads inside to his daughter's bedroom. He has not entered the room for months, and he is surprised by the stillness: the ballet leotards hanging in the closet; the coral blanket on the bed; the child-size dresser; the dollhouse in the corner. It is all preserved, a testament to his daughter's brief life. Fine dust coats the room, and as he brushes some from the roof of the dollhouse, he remembers the gray particles are skin flakes, the last remains of Kata.

He lays Ines on top of the dresser and sees the doll reflected in the mirror. The torso has a dent, a concave bruise. Stumps mark where he sawed the legs all those months ago. He examines the perforation where the nail pierced her body. He goes to his bedroom, to the toy chest where he stores some of his wife's things. After she left, he discarded her clothes, her wedding ring, her empty bottles of šljivovica. He kept samples of her detritus: angular toenail clippings and knots of hair, the algaed mud of a facemask, a trio of her menstrual pads. He takes a tissue imprinted with lipstick and returns to Ines. In front of the mirror, he dabs the tissue against Ines' cheek, but he fails to re-create the tiny red dots.

Silence fills the room, the cottage, the restless parts of his mind. Mislav retreats to his workshop. Beneath the racks of hammers and saws, Mislav traces his finger over the pinkish dust on his workbench. He rubs the soft vinyl matter between his forefinger and thumb, staining his skin. He would like to repair the dolls, bring them back to their pure, original state. He packs a burlap sack with tools, then returns to the house for the dolls.

Back outside, sack slung over his shoulder, he crosses the road into the fields and follows the dirt trail. The land slopes up, the ryegrass thins, wildflowers flourish near limestone outcroppings. His body sways, exhausted. He rests for a while and catches his breath, noting his cottage far below him. He considers going back before darkness falls, but he glances up to the trees, still far off, and knows he must forge on for the sake of the little girls.

He scrambles to his feet, walks stiffly, quartering the land for the trail. Underfoot, the ground feels saturated with meltwater. Winter snow still buries the land at the skyline. A line of crisp white hugs the ridge, and spits of icy snow curl back down the hill, pock the rest of his path. He trudges on slowly. When he reaches the fence, he leans on the rail, breathing hard. Landmines lie beneath the snow in the clearing. He unlaces his boots, strings them to the fence. Then he discards his sodden socks and folds his trouser cuffs above his knees. He runs toward the copse, avoiding every strange area of pitting in the snow. Starlings fly out of the tops of the beech trees. He tracks the birds through gaps in the canopy. They swoop up, wheel around in the sky, then dive out of his view.

Mislav snaps off some low branches, tucks them under his arm. The trees line the crest of the hill. Mislav knows the town sits on the other side, in a broad and flat valley. Kata is buried there, her simple white headstone the same as many others in the cemetery. She would like the quiet down there, and up here, with the trees.

A gentle breeze skitters pale leaves over his bare feet. He can see the brittle lamina, the torn veins of the leaves. He drops all the branches but one, which he breaks over his knee. With his penknife, he whittles the wood into legs for Ines. He glues the roughly hewn cylinders to the vinyl nubs and holds her legs and torso together until set. He does the same for all the little girls. After he redresses the dolls in their frilly dresses and undergarments, he stands each of them in front of a tree, the five girls posed, almost alive.

In the waning light, he looks to the inky mauve sky. Instinctively, as the land darkens, he retrieves the flashlight from his burlap sack and kneels in the misshapen crater. He watches over the dolls, all five of them, scoping the beam of light from one to another. The faces shine. The black eyes gleam. He tells the little girls stories of long ago.

Flight

When the tape runs out, Mara holds the video camera above her head. She tells Patrik to keep dancing. She doesn't want him to learn about her mistake. She had failed to check the length of the tape beforehand. Patrik appears unfazed by her animated insistence, her hand waving in a circular motion. He lifts one knee and flicks his foot. His body pulses forward, then angles up on its toes, spinning around. His arms cross and he crouches down, becoming small and tight like a knot.

She tries to memorize his unrecorded movements. More than thirty years separate them, and she enjoys the youth of his body. He slips effortlessly into a front split and looks to the floor. She focuses the lens on his abdomen, the perfect divots of muscle. She lowers the camera to his black dance belt. Patrik knows little about her relationships with her artist's models, the men she cycles through every few months. He performs so calmly, so unlike a young man. Perhaps he will be the one who can bear her mercurial infatuations. Before she hired Patrik, and long before the eruption of civil war in Yugoslavia, she had fabricated sculpture in plastic and fiberglass. In the seventies, she made her famous series of bird wings, the rectangular blocks molded into *V*'s and bolted into blacked steel pedestals. Back then she became known throughout the art circles of Zagreb and Belgrade for Flight. The critics christened her the heir to Brâncuşi.

Around that same time, she met a shadow version of Patrik at a gallery reception in London. Simon was the only attendee not drinking the free champagne, and she discovered that

he was a ballet dancer. They talked of Makarova, Fonteyn and Nureyev, Nijinsky, of course. The sharp tone of Simon's voice intrigued her as did his knowledge of Hofmann and Rothko. Wearing dark pants and a cream dress shirt, he resembled one of the servers carrying silver trays of petite vol-au-vents and flutes of Moët. But he stood tall, his hair soft and wavy, his long limbs jutting at strange angles. Mara imagined the corded muscle below his clothes and how it could propel his body across the stage and lift a woman with apparent ease. She presumed he was gay but could not detect any of the outward signs. Perhaps she assumed too much about Simon and his reasons for a life in the ballet. Half lost in rumination, she heard him ask something, and she tilted her head to suggest that she was agreeing.

"USSR?" he pressed. "Or Romania? Is that where you're from?"

"It's irrelevant. I'm here now."

"That's one way to leave your past behind."

He was younger than Mara and astute for a dancer; she thought it better to feign ignorance. "I don't understand."

"You shouldn't hide your home country."

"That was not my point, exactly."

"Of course," he said. "It was mine."

Mara struggled to decipher his curiosity about her. She wore an oxblood turtleneck and baggy gray slacks. She was forty-two. Her closely clipped hair was white at the temples. Her face was youthful, boyish. Perhaps he was a tease. He was more handsome than her past lovers, who had been art students—posers, really—without any talent. When she attended the Academy of Fine Arts she studied alongside these men, none of whom were interested in her assemblages of found objects or her experiments with shapes—a mechanistic recasting of natural forms. They lectured her on the aesthetics of the New Tendencies movement while belittling her work as too figurative. They said they would help her, reveal where her art fell short, but usually they tried to sleep with her, which she allowed now and again. In her twenties she embraced celibacy, and she came to the conclusion that she would have to force her way into the art world. She cut her hair short and began wearing trousers and long-sleeved shirts that became flecked with drops of polyurethane. Tiny burn scars marked her hands as she worked with new plastics, perfecting her use of synthetic media.

She suggested to Simon that they look at the rest of the exhibition. They drifted around the perimeter of the room, circling the hundred people in attendance. The gallery contained the work of several Eastern Bloc artists, including hers. Political illustrations hung on the far wall. In one, the artist had depicted Stalin lecturing a group of factory workers from atop a gold hammer and sickle—a moderate dissension. She assumed the man was now in exile in London like so many others. Many of these artists were feted because of their banal political critiques. She disliked the instant and easy attention these men received. As a citizen of Yugoslavia, she was reasonably free to come and go as she pleased. A disfigured portrait of Marshal Tito would mean little outside of a few laughs.

They stopped by one of her pieces, *Flight #8*. With a wingspan of nine feet, it was her largest sculpture so far. The block of fiberglass ran smooth and angular. Coats of white polyester resin and a layer of clear sealant lacquered the monochrome surface. Simon traced his fingertip on the inside of the *V*.

"Be careful," she said. "No smudges."

"This is yours?" He leaned in to read the name printed on the label. "Mara Petrović."

"Correct."

"I thought you were a hanger-on," he said, "like myself."

"I feel like one."

"Do you know anyone here?"

"Just you," she said. "It's rather sad."

"Your sculpture is beautiful."

Mara drained the last of her champagne, wishing a waiter would come by with a second glass. Any distraction from explaining her manifesto on aesthetics. "An interesting interpretation," she replied anyway. "I was going for the opposite."

"Ugliness?"

"More like futility."

"Ah, I didn't get that," he said, like so many of her early critics.

A man she recognized as the curator of the exhibition crossed the gallery floor toward her. His name was Andrew or Duncan—something with two syllables. She had heard from her Zagreb gallery that the curator had inherited a great deal of money from his family and had wanted to ingratiate himself into the arts. Now the man beamed, kissed her cheeks, and asked if she needed anything.

"Another drink," she said.

"Of course," he said, "but first let me introduce you to a few people."

His authority disarmed Mara. Over her shoulder she

saw Simon grin and then become distracted by a man in a white suit. The curator ushered Mara upstairs to a private room, which contained the elite dozen or so of the reception. Several women were chatting over cocktails near the bar, while an impassive barman stood behind a line of expensive spirits and wines. Atop a banquet table sat a chocolate fountain and a cut-glass dish overflowing with strawberries. Robert, as the curator's name turned out to be, said the strawberries had been flown in from the Continent.

As they approached the bar, he ignored the wave of a round-faced brunette. "We've sold two of your smaller pieces," he said. "And I expect to sell the rest within the next month."

"Good. I suppose."

"Are you making more?"

"The Flight series is finished."

"Don't be too hasty," he said. "There are guests here tonight who would love to get their hands on a Petrović."

Robert's insistence turned her stomach. Already she had been planning a move away from the whims of male collectors and critics, leaving behind the comparisons to Brâncuşi and the orbit of his acolytes. Her past obsession with perfectly sculpted biomorphic forms belonged to a different person, who was now foreign to her. In Robert's company she felt this even more acutely, yet she knew she had to play along for now. As she listened to his droning voice, she tried to place his accent, finally settling on South East England, somewhere around Surrey or Kent. She thought of Simon's conversational gambit but regarded a similar move to be wasted on Robert. She masked her distaste for his estimates on how much money she could make and who would buy her sculptures. She drank, and Robert smiled and called a group of his friends over. In a flurry, Mara shook hands with a parade of diamond-clad women and became the center of a discussion about the changeable nature of English weather. Once the small talk was over with, she was pestered with the repeated assertion that she must be glad to be out of a Communist country. She then suppressed a laugh when one of the women asked if people shared art in Yugoslavia or took turns displaying the nation's masterworks.

Mara ate several of the strawberries and drank a third glass of champagne, anything to fade out the chatter of the women. Though she was fluent in English, she felt isolated from their obsessive gossiping about who had been invited and who had been spurned. When Robert abandoned her for a gray-haired man, she made her exit. Downstairs, she hunted for Simon and found him by the bar with the white-suited man and a couple of women in short black dresses. She pressed a napkin into his hand, her address written in purple eyeliner on one side. "Come by," she said. "I need a model."

She photographed Simon in her rented West End flat, capturing the swirls and curves of his non-choreographed rhythms. She envisioned a shift into cut-up representations of the body—a world apart from the fashionable Minimalism of her sculptures. The pictures would be the start. She planned to use a gas oven to melt sheet plastic and mold the semi-molten material with Kevlar gloves. A chance to fix his fluidity in static form. Perhaps half-formed cylinders or misshapen helixes flecked with bubbles and collapsed lips.

Rough, jagged surfaces, that was all she knew.

After they had completed the sitting, Mara poured them each a glass of red wine. Simon sipped his politely and traversed the room. He pointed to the landscape painting on the wall. "I take it this came with the place," he said.

Mara said nothing at first. Watercolors of the English countryside hung in every room, and she felt cheated by the illusion they presented: the rare breaks in overcast skies, the sun illuminating hay bales and meadows, farmers scything corn or tossing seeds into picturesque fields. England was a world away from these genteel pastiches of Constable country. So far she had experienced freezing rain and heavy smog, annoying teenagers on the Tube, and men reading dirty magazines in the library. It was not that different from Zagreb.

"Yes," she said. "And it's priceless." She was glad to see Simon laugh and to have him in her flat. It was not conversation she sought but the possession of another's movements. She took pleasure in orchestrating poses, configuring bodies to her whim. The fetish arose from her time at the Academy when her life-drawing class shared a succession of slight women. She had despised her time spent sketching the models until the professor berated one of the women for moving too often. Mara had felt a thrill that lingered long after the semester was over.

Simon exchanged his wineglass for a film canister on the mantel. "I've never had anyone take so many pictures."

"Not even your parents?"

"Perhaps when I was a child," he said. "I haven't seen them in a while."

"I have a similar relationship with my mother." Mara

stopped herself from revealing any more information; she hated the thought that someone knew something about her family life. "More wine?"

"I have rehearsal in the morning," he said.

"Can you stay longer? I want a few more shots."

"I should get some rest."

"Just one roll," she said. "I can pay for a taxi."

"What do you want me to do?"

Mara directed Simon to crouch by the far wall. She took a light reading of his balled-up body and loaded a roll of Tri-X into her camera. As she stepped close, she wound the film on. She wasted some time fiddling with the lens ring, enjoying the sight of his huddled mass—a helpless boy. Then she was ready to shoot. "Spin up," she said.

Before each session with Simon, Mara rearranged the living room to be a studio. The paintings were taken down and stowed in the closet, white sheets were pinned to the walls, and her Leica was ready on the coffee table. She documented the different sections of his physique: close-ups of forearms spidered with veins, long exposures of bare feet sliding on the linoleum. Once, without explanation, he stood steady, holding his arms by his sides. The stillness terrified her, and she demanded he return to his glissades and jetés and temps levés. Their relationship remained professional, yet they branched out from the sittings to visit museums and movie-theatres, sometimes enjoying a late-night whisky together. They spoke of the art and dance scenes in New York and a mutual desire to see Patti Smith at CBGB. Sometimes Mara probed into his love life, but he always managed to brush her off. Once, when she asked if he had a lover, he told her to leave it alone. In a fit of anger Mara clamped her hand over his mouth and said she decided what he did, who he saw. Simon pulled away and said he was leaving. She noticed he still took his payment from the telephone stand.

Mara lounged in bed, the sheet wrapped around her. She read *Artforum* and half-listened to the news on the radio. Bored by her magazine, she pawed through her photographs of Simon, tracing her fingernail around his stoic face. She saw contempt for her creative process in his contorted expression and in the blankness of his black eyes. Simon had failed to show for his sittings over the last week, and she assumed he was finding money elsewhere.

She shoved the stack of photographs to the floor, reconsidering her ideas about transposing his movements into plastic. She hated her self-doubt; she had always been clear in her vision for her art. The men at the Academy would have enjoyed seeing her falter. She was certain of this.

Later that morning, she set off for the gallery. She hoped she would regain her confidence from viewing her sculptures. Partially, she also hoped Robert would have Simon's telephone number. She had checked the directory but had been unable to find a listing. She assumed that it was kept private from his parents. Now she felt foolish for not having asked him for his number, but relying instead on his regular visits.

The gallery's lobby was empty. No attendant or visitors anywhere. Mara crossed the waxed hardwood floor. Her sculptures had been removed, along with the pieces by the other Eastern Bloc artists. Adorning the walls now were large white canvases, and the paint shimmered in the lines of the dried brushstrokes. Gesso, she surmised. This artist had reduced art to the undercoat—a starkness of form. Against her better judgment, she admired the paintings. She read the label with the artist's name: E. V. Cotterill.

Mara ventured into the annex wing, where she found *Flight #8*. A spotlight illuminated the grandeur of the white-painted fiberglass: the form of a bird that could never fly. In her first conversation with Simon, she had been right about futility. She touched the *V* as he had done. She felt angry and finished with him. But what had he seen in her piece? Beauty, he had said. She tried to look for it in the smooth surface. There was only a faint reflection of herself.

"Mara," a male voice called out. Robert strode across the wooden floor, tufts of black chest hair curling from under his blue paisley shirt. "I'm sorry," he said, taking her hand. "I was going to call and give you an update on the sales."

"That's fine," she said.

"Come, let's have a drink."

A zebra skin spanned the central wall of his office. Beneath it stood a mahogany drinks cabinet, where Robert poured a sherry for Mara and a brandy for himself. She eased herself into the leather chair next to his desk. In the warm glow of his Tiffany lamp, he looked younger than he had the last time: his face now bronzed, his hair dyed at the temples. She thought him silly, a silly old man.

"Your Flight series is almost sold," he said. "And we're still pushing it hard."

Mara doubted the veracity of his statement. She had a feeling her other sculptures were in a warehouse, ready to be shipped back to Yugoslavia. "You need to," she said, "if you want room for those blank slates on the walls."

Robert smiled as he passed her a glass. "Styles come and go."

"I've been working through some new ideas." She sipped her sherry and waited for him to sit in his oversized chair. "But my model is sick. Perhaps you met Simon? He came to my show."

"The dancer?"

"Yes," she said. "I need his telephone number."

"I can get it."

Mara noticed the Rolodex on his desk. She imagined it contained Simon's information and more than he had ever told her.

"He's a popular man," said Robert.

She asked what he meant by that, but he didn't elaborate. Instead he flipped through his ledger and studied the contents of several pages. "You should continue with the Flight series."

"That's over."

"You should reconsider."

"I choose what I make."

"And I choose what I sell."

"In Yugoslavia—"

"We work differently in this country."

She raised her glass and stared at the sherry pooled at the bottom. She smiled in a way she thought would please him and threw back her drink. He laughed and finished the rest of his brandy. As he came around the desk, his countenance appeared jubilant, as though he had locked her into what was to come. He took her glass back to the drinks cabinet. As he fiddled with the bottles, she glanced at the closed door. She wondered if he had a secretary or an assistant of some sort. Even though she hardly knew Robert, she guessed he had a young woman somewhere.

Robert handed her a fresh glass. He sat on the edge of his desk and raised his brandy. "Cheers," he said.

"Ti si šupak."

"What's that?"

"It's the same."

They polished off that glass and then a third. Mara impressed Robert with a few more bursts of Serbo-Croatian, giving him a false translation of each phrase. She secretly reveled in provoking his litany of quizzical expressions. When he excused himself to the bathroom, she considered flipping through the Rolodex herself, but she felt stunned by the alcohol. It had been a while since she had drunk this much. She pushed herself up but sat again when she heard footsteps outside the office. Only a moment later, he was massaging her shoulders. His hands snaked to her chest and fumbled with the buttons of her shirt. For a few seconds she surrendered herself to his touch. She felt sure he was not a terrible lover, and she could imagine herself with him one time. It would not be too bad—most likely rough, sweaty, and short—but when his heavy breaths shuddered against her neck, she slapped his hands away. "No," she said. As she left his office, she could hear his pitiful voice complaining about women, all women.

In the glare of the late-afternoon sun, Mara tried to suppress her nausea. She braced herself against a lamppost, disgusted that she had let a man control her, however briefly. She thought of Simon and his disappearance, which troubled her more than it should. There was a time when men meant nothing to her: they were impediments to her art. She used them when she needed to, that was it. She was unsure of what had changed. Perhaps he had an answer for her. As she walked down the street, a fragment of the name of his studio came to mind. She was convinced it was in Hackney, and she caught a cab.

The studio sat on the corner of a busy junction. Inside, Mara cased the foyer, scrutinizing the show advertisements pinned to the bulletin board. Deeper inside the building, the hallway smelled of dry sweat and some sort of herbal balm. Mara heard shouts from one of the practice studios. A row of young girls stood next to the barre in pink leotards, cream tights, and slim ballet slippers. The teacher was instructing them to unfurl their arms above their heads.

Mara knocked on the mirror and waved to the teacher, who whispered something to the lead girl before coming to meet her. As the woman eased the door shut, Mara tried to describe Simon. The woman said that she knew him, but that was all. "Have you fucked him?" Mara asked. The woman shook her head and told Mara that she couldn't be here, that there were children, young girls, and she escorted Mara to the foyer, where she pointed to a stack of brochures. "Take one," she said. "It has the studio's number."

Mara called the number several times that night and the next day, but her calls went unanswered or were taken by a gruff man who said he would pass on the message. She considered telephoning Robert to get Simon's home number, but she knew he would never give it to her now.

She stayed in the flat and drank wine. One evening, she flipped again through the studio's brochure. Simon's face shone from the pages, his body aloft in midair. The photographer had been given something: the fine edge of a smile. She cast aside the brochure, went out to buy cigarettes, and smoked two as she walked back. Upon entering the flat she took an immediate dislike to the furnishings and tossed out the flower-print sofa cover and the doilies atop the television cabinet. Her eye caught the watercolors on the wall, and she drew dead birds in the fields and blackened the skies with a wax crayon. Then she telephoned the studio and demanded to talk to Simon. When he eventually came on the line, she asked to meet at a local pub.

As she seated herself at the bar, she was unsure if Simon would come. He seemed hesitant on the telephone—his voice soft, his words elliptical. She lit a cigarette and nursed her whisky, resolute that she would leave the pub once it was finished. She waited around a while after her whisky was gone, surprised when Simon showed up and kissed her on the cheek.

His hair was uncombed, a little matted. He could hardly look her in the face. She glanced over to the barman and held up her glass and two fingers.

Simon patted his trouser pocket, then slipped his hand inside, leaving it there. "I'm glad you called. Rehearsals have gotten the better of my time."

"Your ballet must come first," she said.

Mara paid for their drinks, and they moved to a small table in the back corner. They sipped their whiskies and talked about a play they had both seen and then the awfulness of French films. Mara felt she had miscalculated how the evening would go. She had underestimated the degree of his youth and his inexperience in these matters. Her instinct was to lie and make up a pretense for a final sitting. What she knew of Simon, though, was that he was always broke.

"Forty pounds to come back with me," she said.

Simon hooked his fingers around his glass, rotated it, and scraped the bottom against the varnish on the table. "I'd like another."

After she returned with a pair of doubles, he said that he could do with the money, though it would cost sixty.

They caught a cab together. They both smoked rather than talked. Each played mute until they were inside her flat. He asked about the vandalized watercolors in the living room, and she replied that she had been attempting an homage to Duchamp. For the first time he failed to get one of her art references and simply looked around the room, a little lost.

"What happened to your sofa?" he asked.

"I didn't like the color," she replied. "We can sit in the bedroom and have a glass of brandy." She could sense his hesitation from the pause in his breath. "It's special—from my hometown."

They drank the brandy straight from the bottle and then collapsed together on top of the sheets. They lay in the darkness, neither of them saying anything. Then Simon awkwardly undressed. Mara could feel his movements in the bed, and then nothing at all. He didn't try to touch her. She wondered if he had passed out or if he were waiting for something to happen. She turned his way and saw the outline of his naked body and the rise and fall of his chest.

"Let me get the camera," she said.

"I can't do this."

"Just lie back."

"I don't want to."

"Think about anyone you want."

"I have to go," he said. "I was supposed to meet Eric."

"You have to stay."

"No. This is the end of it."

His words barely registered at first, but then her body recoiled and jerked away from his. She stretched over to her purse on the nightstand and groped blindly inside, slapping the pound notes she found against his chest. She left the room. Her mind dizzy, she lay on the blank cushions of the sofa. She listened for any noise in her bedroom, but she could hear nothing. It was possible Simon had fallen asleep or changed his mind about meeting his lover. She raised herself up, a barbed ache growing in her head—she realized that she had met Eric at the gallery reception. It was his paintings that had later replaced her sculptures. She picked up her Leica from the coffee table.

In her bedroom, Simon was kneeling next to the nightstand, the lamp casting his naked body in silhouette. He arched his head around, his mouth opening.

Mara pressed the shutter release, the flash lighting up the room. "Tell Eric to use the money for some color," she said.

"Please, Mara."

"Govno jedno," she said. "Get out."

She took a dozen shots of Simon as he paced around searching for his clothes. He pulled on his trousers and tucked his shoes under his arms. She trailed him into the living room, still taking his photograph. As he left the flat, she flipped the camera around and snapped a picture of her own face.

Winter sun angles through the skylight of Mara's studio, and her gaze flits from the square of glass back to Patrik. Her arms ache from holding the video camera in midair for so long. She draws it to her chest, pretending to refocus the lens. Patrik rises from his pose, and the pale light softens the contours of his muscular torso and angular cheekbones. She knows that, now in her sixties, her past years of working unmasked pinned strands of silica inside her body, which have formed lesions in her lungs. Notwithstanding her illness, she still desires obedience from her young men, like Patrik, though it happens less and less.

Patrik slips on his tracksuit pants and pulls on his T-shirt. She sees his nipples erect through the thin cotton, and she holds in her mind the perfect symmetry of his chest and abdomen. He asks for a cigarette, and she gives him the rest of her pack. Together they exit the studio and wend their way through her narrow gallery. He does not ask about the row of sculpted wing shapes or why she moved on to video. Nor does he ask about her conception of the body or the title for the video installation: *(re)Fracture*. She dislikes the fact that he does not sense what she achieved with the Flight series all those years ago, yet she knows that her latest work will be a chance for her to ascend to her rightful place in the art world. Fame will bless her again.

She passes Patrik an envelope, the front marked with a *P* in her finest hand. The two hundred kuna inside is not as much to her as it is to him. As he accepts the money, he mentions that he cannot make next week's session, as he has rehearsal for *Giselle*. She nods, already resigned to his excuse.

After she watches him hurry down the street to catch the tram on the corner, she goes upstairs to her office. By the computer sits her maquette for *Flight #8*. Silvery hairs glint in the fiberglass. Her fingertip runs up and down the model's valley, the brittle surface now cracked. She never made the sculptures of Simon but instead circled back to Zagreb and Flight, fabricating variations on her earlier pieces. Even now she tries to forget about the box of photographic prints documenting his dances. She is sure Simon must have died of AIDS or Hepatitis B—some disease like that. No matter, there are other men in her life now.

She connects the video camera to the machine, loads the editing software, and observes the film from the tape appear on the computer screen. She speaks into the microphone while playing the sixty minutes of her directing Patrik, narrating his dance until the tape ends and the image dissolves to white. She places her hand over the microphone and slides it down to the base of the stand. Then she presses her lips against the microphone's domed grille and whispers Patrik's last moves: his delicate spin, his balling to the floor. She describes all that she can remember, all that she wants.

Zorana

The duties for Marc's teaching fellowship at Sveučilište u Zagrebu were light. Just a single lecture a week on Russian literature, pre-October Revolution. The university had assigned him a boxy office in the hydrography department. In the afternoons, pale ochre light slanted through the narrow window across the wall map of the Adriatic, and his eye would track the line of sun until he had to switch on the desk lamp. In periods of boredom he flipped through the files in the cabinets, examining the datasets of river discharges and the surveys of unpronounceable glacial lakes. The Black Sea's morphology interested him the most, and he would unfurl the large topographic map to study the three concentric rings, the basin's core at its heart.

It was easy for Marc to stay anonymous in this foreign country. When he paced the university hallways, none of the faculty seemed to know who he was. Perhaps they presumed, because of his youthful skin and Converse sneakers, that he was a student. All semester he had shunned e-mail invitations to dinners and research talks and department cheese-and-wine nights. He preferred his low profile, the solitude it allowed him on campus and in Zagreb. Everywhere he went in the city, he carried a buckskin satchel that rarely held more than his Russian literature anthology and his teaching notes, and a sex magazine in the interior zipped sleeve.

On the final day of class, he went to the Broz Lounge to drink alone. Pretty waitresses worked at the café-bar, and for a few kuna he could drink heavily and give the girls the eye. Since October he had slept with two of the waitresses, but he didn't see them around anymore. He had considered calling them, but other matters, like the end of his fellowship, had pressed on his mind. The last few days he had been wrapping up his stay in Croatia, scouring the online pages of *The Chronicle of Higher Education*, finding a handful of positions in the Midwest. He had dismissed applying for any of the jobs in farm country; instead he was weighing a splurge on a shoestring tour of Europe.

Inside the café-bar, several patrons huddled near a large space heater. Two of the men cursed in low voices about the icy wind whipping through the streets. Marc despised the typical grumblings of old men and their yearnings for the return of Communism, so he sat at the far end of the counter and kept on his winter coat. He took his thick anthology from his satchel. He had half a mind to throw it away. Instead he ordered a beer and used the book as a coaster. The dim lighting and the dark wood paneling of the room reminded him of the terrible sports bars of his hometown. He had barely thought of Holdrege in months. New York had been his city for a decade. First a BA in comparative literature at NYU, followed by a further six years at Columbia—a year longer than he had planned. His parents were unhappy he had abandoned Nebraska, venturing back only for a day or two each Christmas. He had tried to picture them at convocation, in the crowd of clapping parents filling the South Lawn, but they hadn't made the trip. Too expensive, they said.

Marc nursed his beer, thinking of his final months in graduate school a year ago, how his cohort had separated, become lost without the structure of the system. Impressed by the name of his fellowship upon his announcement, they had asked him if the university paid for his flight and apartment. Yes, he had bragged to them, and a lot more. He said all this without disclosing his low stipend or the fact that he couldn't get hired as an assistant professor. The previous semester, during a series of dull hotel room interviews at MLA, several search committees had implied his demeanor was unsuitable for the humanities.

Marc blamed this state of affairs on the recession, on Obama, on the discipline's vacuous interests in digital humanities and pop culture. He didn't sense fault in himself, not exactly. Not in his scholarship, his devotion to Chekhov, however recently diminished. Yet, even in his glum mood, he was curious if the other graduates of his program had achieved more than he had. He scrolled through his university's alumni page on his cellphone and discovered his friend and sometime lover, Anne, had abandoned academia and was now a baker in Park Slope; and Henry, the dolt from the course in Marxist Literary Theory, had secured a tenure-track position at The New School. He worked through the other names he could remember, the inferior doctoral students who voiced ignorant comments during seminars and small-group meetings with his advisor. After tallying up the results, Marc felt aggrieved that he sat in the middle of the curve. He muted his cellphone and ordered another beer.

It was a while before he noticed one of his students at a table in the corner. At least he supposed she was one of his students. In the large auditorium a few hours earlier, he had delivered a riveting lecture on Chekhovian alienation. She had slouched in the front row and stuck in a pair of earbuds, listening to music with an electronic percussive thud. She played with her hair obsessively, using her iPhone as a vanity mirror. Each time he clicked through his PowerPoint slides and revealed an insight on estrangement in Chekhov's fiction, she raked her hand through her sleek bob and smoothed her bangs. Her blonde hair was attention-seeking, he had thought, especially the childish streaks of electric blue. Yet the deliberate weathering of her denim miniskirt turned Marc on, as did the dog-print scarf helixed around her neck, the ends highlighting the curve of her chest. At the pivotal moment of his talk, she had squared a pack of cigarettes on her legal pad and drawn around it with an eyebrow pencil. He could tell there wasn't much holding her back from smoking.

Now, in the café-bar, the woman saw him gawking and she came to the counter and sat on the stool next to his. She whipped off her scarf and laid it across her lap. The outline of a little dog was reprinted all over the swath of pink fabric. Marc took in the fleshy arc of the woman's body. He could clearly see her throat and the tops of her breasts, which crested above the oval neckline of her sweater. She had recently applied thick black eyeliner, her lashes dotted with dark clots.

"Do I know you?" he asked.

"Zorana."

"Interesting name."

"I suppose," she said, placing her purse on the counter. "I'm named after my grandmother."

"The best girls usually are."

"No, just the girls from broken homes." Zorana opened her purse and touched her iPhone. The screenlight illuminated her stash of makeup and a trio of tampons. She fingered her pack of cigarettes and plucked one out as the purse returned to darkness. "So, why were you staring at me?"

"You were in my class today."

"Right," she said. "Your lecture left me full of questions."

"That's good."

"Such as: Did Chekhov think about Olga Knipper?" she asked. "When he masturbated?"

"Just the seagulls. But that's an inside joke."

Zorana laid the cigarette on the counter. "I get the reference."

"That's surprising," he said. "I haven't seen you all semester."

"Attendance is overrated."

"So is pop music."

"I don't listen to pop music. It was techno."

"I'm not familiar with that."

She waved the waitress over. "Buy me another drink, and I'll explain."

Marc ordered another pîvo for each of them, and Zorana dove into a long monologue about electronic dance music and the parallels to primitive tribal dances. By the time she brought up the relationship between repetitive beats and base human desires, he had become bored. He cared for little outside his sphere of expertise, but he nodded now and again, his thoughts drifting to seeing her naked. He imagined a Chinese character tattoo between her shoulder blades, undoubtedly a cheap stand-in for her name or spirit animal. And, he was sure, she was the sort of woman to have barbells pierce her nipples. 12 gauge, at least. Disappointed that her arm covered the front of her chest, he slyly examined the rest of her and guessed she splashed soymilk in her coffee and did yoga when she wasn't hungover.

He glanced up to the flat-screen TV above the shelf of colorful liquor bottles. The news segments had been going back and forth between an approaching winter storm and an EU politician's sexual indiscretion. The hypnotic droning of the newscaster's voice dulled his senses. Marc wanted the television off, and he scanned the counter for the remote control.

"I bet he fucks a prostitute every night," she said. "In his office, too."

"Politics is all seminal fluid," he said. "Analogous, you could say, to Chekhov's stories: a series of inadequate resolutions."

"That's almost an astute observation."

He slid her fresh glass of beer across the bar. He wondered if she could read him, intuit his intent from his lopsided grin or the fidgeting of his hands. "Thank you."

"Do a lot of girls fall for your intellect?"

"One or two."

"That's rather a low number."

His mind ran through his roster, thinking of Zorana. He would have remembered such a name, such a girl. "Are you actually enrolled in my class?"

"I need a smoke," she said. "But I don't want to go to the back."

At the rear of the café-bar was a curtained-off room for smokers unwilling to brave the cold weather. Zorana scrunched up her face and demonstrated how the old men groped her. She touched the small of his back, pressing her nails into the flesh around his spine.

"I'll go with you."

"We might as well go to a hotel."

"Zorana," he said, sensing a challenge. "That's quite the offer."

"I have an honest mind," she said.

"It will hurt you in the end."

"Whatever." She gathered up her cigarette and purse. "I have to make a call anyway."

Zorana went to the beaded curtain. She brushed several strands aside and spoke to someone inside. It irritated Marc that Zorana thought so little of his opinion, that in the years to come she would barely remember him, some American. Once she slipped completely from his view, he stood to leave. He could find another girl. Then the waitress sidled back over. She was pretty, her face angular, pointed. A mole south of her lips resembled a fallen beauty mark. Marc thought her name was Lana. She handed him the copy of *24sata* he had left behind a few days earlier.

"This is yours?" she said.

"Hvala."

"All this writing," she said. "I thought it might be important."

"Very," he lied. That afternoon he had been doing his best at translating the newspaper, suffering his way through the nuances and peculiarities of this strange Slavic off-shoot. Though he was near-fluent in Russian, he struggled with Croatian. He didn't care very much anymore about learning the language; he would be leaving this backwater in a month or two. "Notes for a conference paper."

"You teach at the university?"

"Yes."

"I have seen you on Tkalčićeva Street," she said. "And

here."

"This place helps me relax."

"And the beer is cheap."

"Well, that helps," he said. "So does the pretty waitress."

She laughed and shook her head. She pointed to his anthology. "You shouldn't keep them trapped. The writers."

He moved the pint glass to the counter and flipped through the pages. "So, who have you read?"

"I love Gogol's stories: 'The Portrait' and 'Nevsky Prospekt.' The landscape is so alive and the people so dead."

"Gogol is alright," he said. "But he hated women. And he was Ukrainian. You really need to read Goncharov and Turgenev. Those writers understood the psychology of the Russian state-of-being."

Her fingertips brushed the deckled edge of the book, but then she withdrew her hand and stuck it in her apron pocket.

"Have you taken any classes?" he asked.

"I'm saving my money while I work here," she said. "Next semester I want to go back and finish—"

"Your English is very good."

"Sometimes."

"Your name is Lana, right?"

"Lucija."

"Of course." He ripped out one of the index pages and wrote his number diagonally across the names of twenty dead Russian men. "Call me, Lucija, if you want to talk more about books."

Lucija accepted the page and examined his writing. Her face flushed and she stuck the page into her apron pocket, then she collected the empty glasses and stacked them on the tray. She hurried to the other end of the bar, talking to a woman whom Marc took for a friend. She had short, spiky hair and a gold nose ring. He attempted to make eye contact with both of the girls. Neither reciprocated. Lucija put down the tray, untied her apron and draped it over the register. Her friend came around the counter and they headed through the back office door. He stood to follow them, but the impulse vanished. He would wait for Zorana instead. He closed his anthology and dumped his cellphone on top, refreshing his e-mail to see if anyone had contacted him. No one had, and he started to google Zorana, but he didn't know her last name.

When Zorana returned to the counter a moment later, she slung her iPhone into her purse and snapped it shut. She cocked her head away from Marc and ordered two shots of rakija from a new waitress.

"I don't drink the hard stuff before five," he said.

"The semester is over."

Marc had the urge to say something about the papers he had to grade and the exams he had to prepare for his students. But he knew in her angered state she would see through his lies. His class preparation involved recycling his notes and lectures from graduate school onto index cards. Meta-comments on each read FUCK THE LIFE OF THE MIND or FUCK THE STUDENTS.

The new waitress placed the shots in front of them. She was too old and ugly for Marc's taste, and he stretched out his arm and stroked Zorana's leg. Black hairs stubbled her rough skin. "Were you calling a boyfriend?"

"Perhaps," she said. "How do you feel about Croatian women?"

"I don't understand your question."

"Do you enjoy sleeping with Croatian women?"

"I thought we were on the same page?"

"No. And my question was simple."

Marc lifted his hand and let it hover for a moment, then he stroked her leg again, nicking her skin with his nail.

"I'm doing research," she said, ensnaring his fingers with her own. "When I lived in Switzerland during the war, the Americans were always the ones fucking the foreign girls."

"What's not to like about women?"

"A lot of things." Zorana downed her shot and explained she was completing her master's in anthropology, and she had only sat in on his class because she despised Americans—especially ones so young. She studied the Continental philosophers and rejoiced in the comforts of psychoanalysis and theory. She went on to reveal her big crush on Judith Butler and her ideas about gender performativity. With a blush she admitted her flawless English had originated from her love of American television. Outside of her private high school, she said, she had wasted most of her time watching *Friends*, *ER*, *Will & Grace*. The shows had been a distraction. She glanced down into the well of her glass. "I can't believe you have a PhD."

"I'm thirty," he said.

"And already a professor."

"This is a one-semester gig."

"Then back to the ol' US of A."

"Maybe," he said. "I have no idea."

"So you do doubt yourself. I wasn't sure. You seemed arrogant in class."

"I'm more arrogant in my apartment."

The heat of the tram felt welcoming after the cold walk through Ban Jelačić Square. Licitar hearts attached to the lampposts shone a sickly red. Marc suppressed his laughter over the tacky Christmas tradition. The plastic hearts were strung up throughout the city. Commercialized as much as Coca-Cola.

The tram juddered as it left the stop. Zorana went to the far end of the car and sat in one of the Day-Glo orange seats. Marc hung on grimly to a metal pole near the doors and watched a man on the street steal an ornamental heart from a tree and then swig a mouthful of beer from his bottle of Karlovačko. Snow fell in large clumps, and the man stuck out his tongue to catch snowflakes. He kept his tongue out, snow layering the pink muscle in a semi-translucent white. Marc envied such curiosity with the world. He had spent years researching his dissertation, finally writing over four hundred pages on the narrative structures of Russian folktales. How much he valued his work was unclear to him. Time away from his academic life in New York had shown him he preferred aesthetic pleasures: the experience of women, not books or scholarship.

As the tram curved around the mirrored façade of an office building, he glanced back to see if Zorana was looking his way. She was slouching forward, staring into the glowing screen of her iPhone.

"Hey," he said, slightly disappointed. "Did you see the guy take the licitar?"

"I hate all that heart of the country stuff. It's bullshit."

"We have a similar idea back in the States," he said. "The Midwest as the heartland."

"I don't give a shit about America. Your country has a

bland mindset. A detachment from the rest of the world." She rubbed her forehead with her pinky. The crimson nail polish was chipped.

"Are you tired?"

"No," she said. "I don't want to go home."

Marc walked over and motioned for her to make room. "I thought that was the plan."

"I haven't made up my mind."

He kneeled on the seat in front and faced her. "Is that so?"

"I have heard about you," she said.

"Oh?"

"You have a reputation."

"Only good, I hope."

She laughed. "No. Not at all. But I'm intrigued."

"As you should be."

"Of course," she said. "That's why I followed you."

"So, no coincidence?"

"Coincidences make for bad fiction."

"Indeed, and I read enough in grad school to last a lifetime."

"Do you miss home?"

"New York," he said. "Sometimes."

"I want to leave Croatia. Get a job overseas."

Her phone buzzed. Zorana dipped her head and thumbed off a text. She sent a few more and Marc sat in the seat properly. He considered texting one of his past waitress lovers or calling one of the escort agencies he had seen advertised in his sex magazine. The grainy images of women in bikinis and leather bodysuits, undoubtedly plucked from the web, appealed to his love of surface: the vessel, rather than the soul.

He stared out the window. On the outside of the glass tiny white lines of furred ice splintered into jagged forks. The fractal pattern seemed to go on like this beyond the limit of his vision. He could picture the frost on his childhood bedroom window and his parents calling him downstairs, then telling him not to spend all of his time alone. Not to lug his atlas around with him. Their wheat farm, a clear twenty miles from the outskirts of Holdrege, harbored an anti-intellectual solitude. Books came in a distant third to television and the talk radio out of Lincoln. Winters he hated the most, the acres of dirt hardened under the glaze of slick ice, evenings spent filling the storage bins with an endless stream of grain.

The tram trundled into a block of grand apartment buildings. Snow had blanketed parked cars and the blacktop. Fresh tire tread patterns cut through the vista of white, leaving dark lines that blended at the intersection. There was no one on the street. "This is my stop," he said.

"Well, let's get off."

They alighted from the tram and stopped at a kiosk for her to buy a pack of cigarettes. He twirled the carousel of postcards, searching for a good picture of the cathedral. In the glare of the streetlight, the images looked worse than the ones he had taken with his cellphone. He had e-mailed snapshots of the Manduševac Fountain and the statue of King Tomislav to Anne and included pithy taglines. Her only response had been: *I hate you. Don't contact me again.*

Zorana nudged his shoulder. "Are you buying one?"

"I wouldn't know who to send the card to."

"A girlfriend?"

"Are you offering?"

"You're very forward for a professor."

"Does that bother you?"

"Men are like that here. They take what they want."

"I'm not going to rape you."

"Of course not." She ripped off the plastic sheathing her pack and flung it over her shoulder. "I could tell that from your lecture."

"What was wrong with it?"

"Derivative," she said. "Your words were the same as the book."

Marc bristled at her suggestion that he was some sort of fraud. He put aside a moment of roiling anger and remembered why he had brought her here: her short skirt, her long legs leading to silver high heels. The nuances of her self-imposed aesthetic, graduate student who cared but didn't care, a hipster attitude he hadn't seen much of over here.

"You're a tease," he said. "I enjoy that."

"I wasn't always."

They walked on, and she smoked. The snow had let up, but Marc still felt cold. The wind chilled his face, the skin numbed as if it belonged to someone else. He asked Zorana for a cigarette. She didn't appear to hear him—she looked to the sidewalk as she recounted the history of her family in the east, near the Serbian border. She detested the village in which she had grown up. Fields of ryegrass flanked the family house and there had been a sick draft horse her father used for tilling. And shrikes, so many of the strange carnivorous birds. Her memories centered on the stink of sausage drying in the attic, the foul odor of dried blood drifting into her bedroom. Fumes from the dead meat infiltrated her bedsheets, her best dresses, her skin and hair. Shrikes were attracted to the scent and inhabited so many parts of the farm. She was glad of the war, that the Serbs shelled the village and that she got the chance to leave. But then her father had fought for the JNA.

"He broke up the family," she said. "My mother was ashamed."

"You've seen him since?"

"Never."

They crossed the street and headed down an avenue lined with tall spindly trees, the black trunks pitted with snow. A fresh volley of flurries blew across the cobblestones. Marc huddled up, and Zorana leaned into his shoulder. He grabbed her hand, feeling resistance at first, but then she held on even tighter. He pictured her as a child, a waif with bleached-white skin and ash blonde hair—her nostrils flaring as she smelled butchered flesh and saw shrikes perched on the roof of the smokehouse.

At the building on the corner, he said, "This is me."

She glanced up at the scrolled eaves and flicked her cigarette in the air. They both watched the burning stub fly into the road. He unlocked the door, and she followed him up one staircase, then another. She pushed out heavy breaths tainted with tobacco. Amused by her wheezing, he said, "Almost there."

Inside the apartment he pointed out the grimy stucco walls and laughed at the stink of the pork ćevapi he had eaten for lunch. Zorana grimaced and crossed her arms. Marc called the place his dacha—an inside joke with himself—but he didn't want to share the nickname with Zorana.

Instead he speculated aloud that the interior had last been remodeled sometime in the Communist era. A purple velour sofa dominated the living room, and he sat on the edge of the armrest. He faced the boxy television set, which received six or seven channels.

"I thought you'd have a nicer place," she said.

"It's a rental," he said. "Where do you live?"

"In Novi Zagreb, with two other girls." She squinted at the airport novels on the coffee table as though she were translating the titles. "My father doesn't give me money anymore."

"Neither does mine."

"Very funny."

"It is a funny situation," he said. "My father grows wheat, but he never makes any money. Just enough to pay the bank back each month."

"You're a farm boy. I suspected as much."

Marc ran his hand through his hair. "And you're a farm girl."

"So we shouldn't have kids," she said, laughing.

"That right?"

"You're too good-looking in that wholesome American way."

"I do have good teeth."

"You're not wholesome, though, are you?"

He crossed the room to the rectangular archway. His bedroom was down the dark hallway. "How about a tour?"

"How about we sit on your awful sofa?"

"Sure," he said. "But first a drink."

"Just a glass of water."

"Any vodka with that?"

"Water's fine. No ice."

He went to the kitchen and surveyed the counter for some clean glasses. He caught sight of the calendar on the refrigerator. A picture of a frozen waterfall depicted the month of December. There were three weeks of exams until the end of the semester. He had circled Christmas Day some time ago, when he stole the calendar from his office. He had no intention of flying to Nebraska. He thought only of a stylish hotel on the Mediterranean now as he filled two tumblers with vodka and sloshed in a couple of ice cubes.

When he returned to the living room Zorana was on the sofa, her knees tucked under her chin. Her silver high heels had been kicked to the floor. She took the glass, exchanged it for the remote on the side table and flipped through the channels. She paused on an episode of *Buffy the Vampire Slayer* and cranked up the volume. Dubbed voices sailed through the room. The plot, as best Marc could make out, hinged on the discovery of body parts in a locker. Athletic teenagers ran through a hallway fighting a host of colorful demons. Blunt weapons pierced vital organs.

They watched the first third of the show before his boredom drove him to make a move. He shifted closer and jammed his tongue in her mouth. She bowed her head. She apologized, then said it was okay to keep going. He unlooped her scarf and playfully bit her nape and licked the length of her clavicle. Her body bucked, then stiffened. Her legs twisted. She kissed him back, like he was that stupid Angel character, and he pawed at her breasts. To his disappointment, her nipples were not pierced. She guided his hand to her inner thigh and squeezed the fleshy part of his palm. He unbuttoned his fly and yanked down his jeans so she could get a good hold on him. She wrapped her scarf around the base and tugged the shaft for three or four strokes, then her grip went slack.

"I remember this episode," she said. "It just came to me."

"This show is garbage. Turn it off."

"No, this is a good one."

"Fuck TV."

"Fuck you." She jerked back her hand and wiped a glob of clear liquid on her skirt.

Marc untangled the scarf and hitched up his jeans, annoyed at her for leading him on. He went to the kitchen to grab another drink. The vodka bottle was empty. In the cupboard he found an ex-lover's bottle of watermelon schnapps. He uncorked the liqueur and drank until the sickly alcohol coated his throat. He leaned against the refrigerator door and listened to the din of the television. The voices were muffled, a man talking to a woman. An aging couple. His finger touched the 25 of Christmas Day, and he remembered the last year he had lived on the farm, and the Christmas morning he argued with his parents about his move to New York. He had told them not to call or write.

His parents didn't understand him. They couldn't accept his desire to leave and pursue something separate from them. They were wrong, and so was everyone who had ever doubted him. There was a woman in his apartment. Women sought him out. They always found him, whatever he said or however he acted. They needed him. Anne had. And so had the waitresses at the Broz Lounge. And now Zorana.

Doubt suddenly plagued him. He imagined her already out of his apartment: a blur of pale flesh running down the street away from him; she would go home and write up her notes and detail how the largess of late capitalism had corrupted academia, and quote Jameson and Butler, and throw in some Žižek for good measure. Marc would become her case-study. Then, with every behavior diagnosed and psychoanalyzed, in the coming months she would complete her master's thesis, and apply for jobs anywhere but her home country.

She would leave.

He ripped the calendar off the refrigerator door and threw it toward the trash can. The pages broke apart and fluttered wildly in the air. Scenes of idyllic sandy beaches and meandering oxbows and vistas of red and brown leaves landed scattershot on the linoleum. He kicked the pages into a makeshift pile before rejoining Zorana. She was sitting cross-legged in front of the television, touching the screen. Blasts of snow rattled the windowpanes, and when she saw the blizzard, she turned up the volume. He lay on the sofa and raised the bottle of schnapps to one eye, watching her and the *Buffy* rerun through the green glass. He found it gratifying that she was still here, waiting for him. That her future was uncertain. Their lives outside of his apartment were not yet determined, not now, and wouldn't be until the morning.

Fatherland

Winter storms follow our Range Rover down the rutted gravel road. Across the land, snow squalls have blanketed this part of Slavonia and vanished away any sign of a farmhouse. Next to me, my young son sleeps, his body strapped to the seat. I cruise the vehicle along, slow, as not to wake him. I am searching for the fields where I worked with Antun and my half-brother Juraj. Twenty years have elapsed, and the farmland looks the same, though it was not winter when I was last here. Now a crust of ice slicks the stubbled fields and loose snow blows across the road. The sun is low in the sky, at our back, the light breaking through the gray cloudbank.

Farther down the road, past a great bend, the GPS tells me I have arrived. I pull onto the berm next to a wooden field gate and keep the engine running, let the hot air from the blower warm my son. Back home, my wife must wonder what is taking so long. This detour will add several hours more than I usually take to visit my mother. She dotes on my son, Filip. They play games and sing nursery rhymes. They look at old family pictures to see who we used to be. But all that will not be enough to explain the time discrepancy.

I smooth my son's thatch of blond hair and kiss his forehead. His skin feels clammy—a remnant of his recent bout of flu. He stirs, and a sleepy gurgle comes from his mouth. "Back soon, my son."

I climb out and open the hatch. I pocket the trowel, and I heave the metal-detector upward so the loop rests on my shoulder. Snow covers the hills in the distance. I shield my eyes and scope the fields for the burial site.

When the three of us were barely teenagers, the land before us squared into fields of maize and barley and sunflower. Hills abutted the far edge of the fields, and we knew somewhere on the other side lay the border with Republika Srpska. We had gathered by the barbed-wire fence to dig an irrigation canal for Antun's father. We studied the line of pegs in the ground. The proposed route of the irrigation canal ran parallel to the fence before veering off and disappearing up a gentle slope. We spat on our hands and rubbed them together. Standing in a line, we thrust our spades into the dirt, shoveling out clods of heavy brown earth. As we piled the clay soil onto the bank, we joked about skipping school and our boring history lessons on our country.

All morning we worked, yet we carved out just a few feet of shallow ditch. Our thinly muscled shoulders ached. Our lips and tongues dried from the overhead sun. Sweat slicked the smalls of our backs, the crooks of our legs. We complained to one another about the length of the irrigation canal. We dug until our hands could no longer grip the spades. The handles left our skin chafed and red like our fathers'. A day earlier, we had assumed we would be finished by now. We thought we would be rich off a few hours of labor. Antun's father had sold the job to us this way. He told us we would be soldiers, protectors of the land.

Antun defended his father roping us into the work for Hrvatska. It was true the country needed rebuilding after the war, that the borders were still vulnerable. At school, the teachers said the same things. At least there we could rest our heads on our desks or play truant in the bathrooms. This oversized ditch was going to take us the rest of the semester.

No soldier of the HV would benefit from an irrigated field. In protest, we propped the spades against the fence and sat cross-legged with our lunch sacks. We unfolded the wax paper sheathing our meat-paste sandwiches. We grimaced at the taste of chicken liver and washed down the mashed entrails with our canteens of sickly orange Cedevita. Our mothers had packed us slices of apple savijača and uštipci choked with kajmak. At home, our mothers worried about our futures, but our fathers did not care. They sat in armchairs and drank rakija and watched TV, and in the evenings they left to smoke with friends in the café-bars. They were ex-everything: ex-mechanics, ex-police officers, ex-sanitation workers. They were ex-husbands and ex-fathers.

Since my mother moved north to Virovitica, I have had no reason to visit this part of the country. I am a dutiful son and visit my mother often, bringing Filip and a jar of her favorite sour cherries. She tries to feed me odojak cutlets or veal šnicle. I decline, say I have dinner planned with Jelena. My mother can barely stand my wife, says Jelena is strange for being vegan. I abstain from telling my mother that I, too, do not eat meat. This morning I helped her sort through some of my father's possessions and box them up for me to take. Amid the process, she discovered empty brandy bottles and cassette tapes of Juraj's singing and funny sketches of Miłošević in my childhood notebooks. I laughed, and in this way, distracted her from talking about Juraj or the diary entries I had written about my father.

Even as I leave my son behind in the vehicle, it seems clear I want to shake these fragments of my youth, unburden Filip of my past. In my pocket rests Antun's letter. Until today I had no idea he remembered me. I seldom spoke to him during my studies at the gimnazija, and I sensed he understood I had befriended him to get some paid work. After that summer I rarely saw Antun. Once in a while I glimpsed him in the fields as my mother drove us past. A few years later, I left for the University of Rijeka to study mathematics. There I met Jelena. I was instantly attracted to her seriousness and her desire to raise a family. After graduation we got engaged, and I performed my civil service at the Pension Insurance Institute. Around the same time, the HV conscripted Juraj. He stayed in the Army after he completed his compulsory period, finding comfort in the routine and discipline. For my generation, Juraj's choice was the patriotic one. I was viewed as a bean-counter, a man who played it safe. In contrast, my relatives made only one distinction between us: Juraj's father was a member of the League of Communists, and mine was a lazy drunk. Yet it was I who went on to have a career, unlike Juraj. After his discharge, he turned to marijuana and amphetamines, and finally heroin.

When my mother pressed Antun's letter in my hand this morning, I thought it was a prank. For a long time I had assumed I had imagined the events of twenty years ago: that afternoon a dream or conjoining of memories. But Antun's letter recounted our actions, and what I had made him do. He blamed me more than Juraj. I was the older brother, after all, and I had spoken for both of us. Antun said in his letter that he became a recluse, a solitary boy, a loner who worked on the farm and took it over when his father died. He never married. He thought of me, he wrote, every season, every color change in the fields. I did not believe his story or the veracity of his obsession. He had to be lying. I was not a bully. I had not ruined his life. No mention of that day could be found in my childhood diary. I looked for other records of that time and came across my father's old metal-detector. I knew I could use it to prove that what Antun had said was untrue.

Beyond the gate, a dirt track runs into the fields. As I clamber over, the metal-detector slips from my grasp and lands on the frozen mud. I curse under my breath, scoop up the metal-detector, and make my way down the track. Angular sunlight reveals a combine's tire tracks ribbed in the mud. I turn back toward the Range Rover and glimpse the dark outline of my son. His body is still—I hope that his mind is unconscious in this moment, that he will not come to remember today. I look away. The cold of the encroaching storm is settling in, so I button my peacoat and upturn the collar. I walk on, faster now. Less than an hour of light remains.

By the time the three of us returned to work that afternoon so long ago, the sun had migrated behind dark thunderheads and the maize swayed in the wind. Raindrops soon pelted the tops of our heads, so we ran to the silo and waited out the storm beneath the conical hopper. Lightning marbled the sky, and thunder rolled through the valley. We squatted on our haunches and teased Antun. We told him to hold the hopper's struts, that he would feel electricity glide over his body like a woman's hands.

Antun's face reddened, and he looked at the ground. We wondered if he was old enough to know what we meant. He was the youngest—thirteen, to our fourteen and fifteen. He wanted to go home, but his family's farmhouse sat a distance away, in the shadow of the border hills.

While he stood quietly, we darted back and forth from the silo, each time running farther away. Rain thrashed the fields, and we shouted to the sky for the lightning to strike, to bring our deaths. We challenged Antun to join in. When he refused, we knew he was no longer part of our trio. We grabbed his arms and wrenched him from his place of safety. He kicked at us, yelled for us to stop. He looked ready to cry. We tossed Antun into the wet mud and ducked back underneath the hopper, laughing at him when he joined us and cowered on the concrete base.

Once the thunderstorm passed, we went back to the irrigation canal. We stood atop the bank and cursed the water that had swamped the ditch. We bickered over which one of us should have brought along a tarpaulin.

"Not me," said Antun.

"Then your father."

"This is our job."

"So?" we said. "We're going home."

"My father won't pay you."

"We'll take the money from you."

"You can have my share," said Antun.

As Antun looked on, we used our canteens to bail out the murky water. At the other end of the ditch lay a bird of prey. Mud slicked its short wings. The bird appeared dead, and we used a spade to scrape it up the bank. The bird had a bluish hue to its feathers. Antun identified it as a sparrowhawk. The bird bucked and opened its hooked bill, shrilling a brittle screech. Antun fumbled with its body and sharp talons, trying to sit the sparrowhawk upright against a fencepost, finally letting it lie flat. Close to death, the bird still eyed us, its yellow irises ringed with milky bands. We argued over whether lightning had struck the sparrowhawk or if it had flown too close to the ground. We laughed. We cared little for how the bird had become injured. We cared for how we would spend our money. And Antun's share.

All these years later, I work in finance. My wife likes my job and its benefits, but I abhor my days there. The work is safe and repetitive and meetings with the analysts take up most of my mornings. Here, in the fields, the temperature is below freezing, and I can feel my face numb. My cellphone buzzes and I switch it off, sure it is my wife. I will tell her later that the storm interfered with the reception. I hate lying to her, but for my peace I must resolve Antun's accusation that I set his life on a self-destructive path, marooning him here in the farmlands. I wish Juraj could have confirmed the details of that day, but he is lost like my father.

For so long our family has been broken. Only with my marriage to Jelena and the birth of our son has this branch of Marković begun to redeem itself. The contents of Antun's letter exaggerate our childish horseplay. We were young, after all. No more than boys making sense of our place in the world.

Before me, threads of copper light illuminate the snow on the hills and throw the ridge into relief. The silo's aluminum shell glints at the end of the track. As I trek over, I can just make out a farmhouse near the horizon. No lights are on. But Antun is sure to be studying me through binoculars, enjoying my struggle in the cold. I wonder if he wants me to suffer, to relive his pain. I can almost hear his voice, his whispers gathering in the snowstorm.

I sit on the silo's concrete base and read Antun's letter again. It should have been me who killed the sparrowhawk, he argues, not him. I do not understand why he says this. I do not remember how the bird died, only that we covered its body with a spade. Even so, I cannot work out the connection between the sparrowhawk and Antun's subsequent life. Antun is a liar. Or he is mistaken. Deluded. I am unsure which. I ball up the letter and throw it in the direction of his farmhouse. Then I head to the corner of the field where the fence has collapsed. At a patch of ground that seems familiar, perhaps once an irrigation canal, I don the headphones and sweep the metal-detector over the dirt. Blitzes of static crackle in my ears. I follow the fence line and guide the detector to the best of my memory. Among shards of glass and split pegs, I locate a broken tilling disc. I circle, trying to find the remains of the spade in the fading light.

The sparrowhawk lay twitching beneath the barbed-wire fence. Antun sat near the bird. He watched the quick rise and fall of its chest.

"You should wring its neck," we said.

Antun shifted his body, his hands raised toward us. "If we find it some food, another bird, it might live."

"We can't save it," we insisted. "Let's get drunk instead."

We brought out our bottle of rakija, stolen earlier from our mother's house. We each knocked back a mouthful before handing the plum brandy to Antun. He sniffed the lip, then drank some. We stepped around him while he drank some more, and we kicked the sparrowhawk into the ditch. Before Antun knew it, we had plucked the bottle from his grip. Eagerly we guzzled more: our stomachs warmed, our minds fizzed. We sat on the bank, dangling our feet over the sparrowhawk. Its feathers shone in the sunlight. The bird half-extended one wing and flapped weakly, as if it could fly away over the hills.

Antun heaved up a spade, held it against his chest. "You shouldn't have done that."

We tilted the bottle, threatening to pour brandy over the bird's head. "If you don't end its life, we'll drown it."

"I'll tell my father."

"And he'll do what?"

"Talk to your mother, your fathers."

We threw the bottle at Antun's feet where it shattered in the dirt. We shunted him out of our way and pried jagged glass from the ground, waving the shards near his face. We told him to be careful of what he said. Antun began to cry; urine soddened his jeans. He ran around us and stood above the sparrowhawk, his arms shaking as he wielded the spade. We thought that he would throw it down—that he would run home. We did not expect his sudden decision. He struck the top of the bird's spine. The sparrowhawk let out a soft squawk. His second strike hit a wing, cutting off a feathered length of tendon and bone. The bird lay unmoving in the mud, its neck mostly severed. Dark blood streaked down over the tip of its bill. One last breath rippled the pool of shallow water. A single glassy eye stared at us, at me.

A series of high-pitched beeps sound in my headphones, and I wrest them off and toss aside the metal-detector. Kneeling,

I brush away a layer of frozen dirt, looking for a sign. A rectangular imprint colors the soil, and I retrieve the trowel from my pocket and stab the point into the ground, angling out crisp divots of earth. I hack away until the trowel handle cracks. Instantly, I sink my hands into the dirt and claw out the heavy clay soil. As I dig, my nails blunt and splinter. I keep going though I can no longer feel the tips of my fingers. At last I come across the steel blade of the spade and pry it out.

In the dirt below, I find an array of tiny bones, separated and fractured, some hacked into fragments. A little deeper, I uncover a small white oval the size of a child's fist. My bruised fingers are raw and blue, and I balance the tiny skull on my palm. I raise the skull, the dark sockets inches from my own. Fracture lines run across the base of the skull. Across the fields, I hear a voice cry out—my boy has awakened. He is cold and missing me. But he must hold on. I will not be too much longer. Above me the sky is matted with snow clouds, and I scan the land for the road and my vehicle. The fields are silent and gray in the scrim of dusk. I strain to see the way I came. I make a guess of where my boy is, and I start the long walk back.

Darkroom

The air is different here, in this new life of hers. Ana knows the perception is temporary, a relief from the suffocation she felt before moving to Zagreb. For now, while she sits inside the darkness of her newsstand kiosk, she watches the returning soldiers across the square. They troop toward the central train station in the indigo light of dusk. Spotlights bolted to the ornate concrete façade shine downward, illuminating a world of angular faces, skin taut and slate gray. The soldiers disappear through the station arches—she counts them, one by one. She fingers the Rolleiflex under her thick winter coat, belted to her naked belly so the camera will not slip. She rations her film, sticks to eight shots a day. While she waits for the right moment, she remains on her stool, the odd bulge hidden below the counter.

From her vantage point, Ana can photograph any of the commuters walking past. She prefers to take close-ups of patrons who steal from the kiosk, usually a magazine or a bar of nougat. She covertly encourages them—she waits silently in the dark, her presence barely discernable within the boxy structure. After a short while, a greasy-haired man leans over the counter. She shrinks into the corner, pleased the man cannot reach the cigarettes. As he withdraws his arm, she aims the twin-lens camera through the fabricated holes in the coat's lining and presses the shutter release.

That evening, after her shift is over, she sets the camera on her nightstand. One of her lovers wants her to take nude pictures of him. "Artistic images," Grgur offers. Ana spurns his suggestion. The previous day she had refused to stow the camera in the drawer for her other lover, Henrik, who was paranoid Ana would send photographs to his wife.

From the bed Ana eyes Grgur's sunken chest, the contrast with his fatherly potbelly and mound of silvery pubic hair. The age gap between them means something to him, a victory of sorts, but it means little to her. She lights a cigarette and takes a drag. He asks again if she will take his picture.

"It's a waste," she says.

"We ought to be celebrating."

"You didn't fight."

"I did my part."

"Nothing worth a picture."

Grgur pulls on his grubby underwear and slacks in an exaggerated manner. Then he leans down next to her; his heavy-lidded eyes try to gaze into hers. "My wife is more adventurous," he says. "And she's old."

Ana ashes her cigarette against his cheek. Grgur jerks back, pawing desperately at the smudge of burning ash. "Kurvo," he says. He throws on his workshirt and jacket, leaves her flat in a rush.

Ana goes to the window and watches Grgur run up the block for the tram. She feels unsure of how much longer she can bear to stay in Zagreb. Since her father's death a year ago, she has been slipping between lovers and cities, switching jobs so no one knows her for very long. She taught for a while at her hometown school before being dismissed for striking a young girl. Prior jobs at a nursing home and a veterinary clinic ended similarly. Romantic triangles distract her from such matters and allow her to temporarily enjoy, as she does, the jumble of limbs. But lately she has grown tired of men and their selfish needs.

Ana returns to the nightstand and extricates the roll of film from her camera, sealing it inside a canister. She slips on her winter coat, partially buttons it, then picks up her Rolleiflex. She exits her flat to visit the pharmacy at the end of the street. At the counter, Ana hands the assistant the canister and asks her to develop it immediately. The assistant bristles at Ana's tone, but then she seems to take in Ana's half-open coat, the expanse of bare skin now on show. The assistant opens the drawer next to her and takes out a roll of Tri-X, placing the film on the counter. Ana scoops it up and sits in front of the large plate window and listens to the hum of the film processor. She knows she will break it off with Grgur and Henrik; the unpleasantness of each man has taken its toll, and she feels ready to be alone again. She loads the new film into her camera, soon aware of shadows fluttering on the other side of the glass. The pharmacy's fluorescent light washes over a group of drunken revelers. One of the men, in a gaudy purple tracksuit, laughs when he spots Ana. He comes to the window and grabs his crotch. He spits a few words under his breath. Ana stands, unfazed by this stranger. She runs her fingers down the front of her coat and fools with the buttons, exposing herself. "Is this what you want?"

The grin disappears from the man's face. He glances around, then rejoins his friends across the road. Ana imagines he is a soldier, or ex-soldier, of the Hrvatska Vojska. The recent end of the war means little to Ana—her father did not live to see it. Both of them had distrusted the virulent patriotism that swept Croatia, the array of flags and graffitied slogans that proclaimed *Za dom spremni!*, the hatred for the Serbs. She sits back down and wedges the camera in her lap, wiping the two lenses with the hem of her coat.

A while later the assistant emerges from the back room and calls Ana over. Ana unseals the packet. All twelve pictures center on the men. Their faces look grotesque and stiff and lifeless. She rips the stack in half and dumps the pieces in the trash basket. Leaving the pharmacy, she heads out of her neighborhood. She photographs a series of haloing lampposts and wet cobblestone streets, silhouettes of women on street corners. Beneath constellated light she explores the edge of Old Town, drifting into Donji Grad, her instinct drawing her to the birds nesting on the banks of the Sava River. She walks along a dirt path in the darkness. After a while, she flops down on the riverbank and takes in the course of the black, glassy water. She hardly cares if she falls in, her whole body submerged beneath the surface. She remembers that in the aftermath of the first ceasefire she went on a birdwatching trip with her father. They hiked to the cratered lake on the outskirts of Imotski and photographed pratincoles and swallows and all manner of plovers. Then they inched to the crater's edge and stared at the water far below. As the sun hit the horizon, her father promised Ana the Rolleiflex after he passed away.

Before the end of winter, Ana converts her bedroom into a darkroom. She buys a secondhand enlarger, bottles of developer and fixer, plastic tubs, a red light bulb. She tapes black cardstock to the windows and invests in thick velour drapes. For hours, in the cold evenings, she develops her films and prints off the black-and-white pictures. Most are fogged images of tired male faces, gaunt features, cigarettes hanging on thin lips. In the background of several snapshots the same woman appears near the sign for the train station.

The woman wears a slick leather jacket, a knit hat, her hair poking out the back. She looks to be in her mid-fifties: her hard face sculptural and striking. Somehow she only seems real by the pair of moles below her lips.

In her darkroom bed, Ana thinks of the woman and her distinctive gaze. The woman always seems to be waiting for someone, a lover or dealer. Perhaps Ana herself. She has no memory of seeing the woman in person; the woman exists on her negatives, in her prints, a presence she cannot feel or sense beyond the glossy surface. When Ana wakes in the blood-red glow, unsure of the time or her location, the woman's face lingers, a ghost-image before her.

At the start of her evening shift, Ana pretends to tidy the carousels of postcards that flank the kiosk. She riffles through historic landmarks of Yugoslavia: Mljet's salted lakes, the Narodni muzej Srbije in Belgrade, a panoramic view of Dubrovnik. Her father had talked about his trips to places like these. Sometimes, he mentioned the women he met. As a child, she would listen to his soulful accounts of their bodies. His descriptions sounded like elegies, flesh he would never revisit. Afterward, he pressed gifts on her: onyx earrings, a single champagne flute, a leather-bound diary stamped with a woman's name. In the following years Ana had come to the unpleasant conclusion that her father had stolen the objects from his lovers.

Later in the night, tucked safely inside the kiosk, Ana clutches her favorite of the postcards. She thumbs the matte surface: the hillside image has faded in the days of sun. The muddy off-color appears little different to her view of passing workers, gradations of polyester gray. Then a man stands in front of the kiosk. He wears a HV uniform and patrol cap, a rifle slung over his shoulder. He pockets a copy of *Sportske Novosti*. She takes his picture. He looks up after hearing the whir of the shutter. He pitches the newspaper at Ana and calls her a kurva. As he walks away, she releases the camera from the belt and tracks his image to the station. In the viewfinder, she sees a blurry version of the woman leaning against a lamppost, smoking a cigarette. Ana focuses the lens. The woman slips from view, disappears into the crowd.

For the rest of her shift, Ana watches for the woman. She saves her film. She has three frames left, but that may not be enough to get a clear shot. She could show a picture to the other vendors near the station. Someone must know her. Ana ruminates on the identity of the woman over the course of the night, her mind drifting into a kind of half-sleep. Behind her eyelids she sees walls of gray fall away to reveal the woman standing over her. The woman's face is smooth, featureless, coated with a layer of shiny plastic.

Ana startles awake. There is no one on the street. She feels lightheaded, shaken, her throat tight. She shutters the kiosk and leaves. Outside the station, she can hear the electrical buzz of the overhead cables, the last tram of the night speeding away from her. She heads down the boulevard, toward her flat, trying to forget her vision of the woman.

Ana stops at the pharmacy on her street. An assistant sweeps the floor inside. Ana raps on the window.

The assistant looks up. "We're closed."

Ana presses her lips against the glass—a shiver of cold radiates through her skull. She asks for sleeping pills.

The assistant lifts her broom, lets the stiff bristles hover above a pile of dirt. "Do you have a prescription?"

"I need to sleep."

"I can't help you."

"Just give me a pill for tonight."

"Try milk with brandy." The assistant goes behind the counter and flips a switch. The pharmacy blinks to black.

The monochromatic haze of Ana's late shifts blur into a single continuous night. Faces appear warped, masklike, grafted from one body onto another. Though she still carries the camera with her, she has not taken any shots in days. She feels so tired she stays seated on her stool. Her weary eyes lock onto the postcard of the hillside: the landscape seems familiar, a lost fragment of her childhood. She stuffs the postcard into her coat pocket and half closes her eyes. A knot of people gloss by the kiosk. Ana tracks their path toward the train station. One thin figure in a black jacket breaks from the group and stands beneath a lamppost; she taps a pack of cigarettes against her palm. Ana recognizes the woman from her pictures. She opens her coat and checks the viewfinder: the woman is there. Ana exits the kiosk and crosses the road to the woman.

"You've been watching me," says Ana.

The woman lights her cigarette; she says nothing. Scuff marks age her leather jacket, her lacy blouse underneath soiled with grease spots. Ana can smell the woman's rank odor. She is taken aback by the woman's heavily weathered face and the white roots showing at her hairline.

"I don't have any business with you," the woman says.

"Tell me what this is about."

"Get away from here."

Ana strikes the woman on the bridge of her nose. Instantly blood ribbons over her lips, the tip of her chin. Somehow the cigarette hangs at the corner of her mouth. Ana slides a hand under her winter coat and presses the shutter release. The woman draws the bloodied cigarette from her lips and holds it before her. She steps back and flees toward the train station. Wanting another shot, Ana cranks the winding lever around. The film is jammed, so Ana chases after the woman. Ana slips off the curb and falls onto the road. She feels a flash of pain in her back and lies there, waits for it to dissipate. Then she sees her coat has come fully open. Male voices shout urgently about cameras, sexual perverts, criminals, Serbian spies. Ana gropes for the Rolleiflex, which has come unbuckled from the belt. She tilts the camera back, makes sure the dual lenses are undamaged. A crowd gathers around Ana. They grasp for the camera; they paw at her face. She struggles to pull herself up. When she gets to her feet, she shoulders through the scrum of men. She hurries to the kiosk and fastens the glass security screen and flips off the light. For a while she remains still, her mind uneasy. She knows her time working in the kiosk is over. She reattaches the camera, then cinches her belt. She waits for the line of soldiers to cross the square.

Before long a tram rattles to the stop near the station arches. Ana heads out and hops the tram. She sits at the back of the car and rests her forehead against the square pane. Concrete buildings flit by in a cloudy haze.

At her flat, she drinks a shot of rakija in her kitchen. As she clutches the bottle, she catches her reflection in the colored glass and looks away. She searches her pockets for the postcard, but it is gone. Part of her wants to return to the kiosk and the street, but she knows the postcard is lost, swept away with the rest of the city's trash. She takes another swig to ease her pain. After drinking some more, she decides to develop her last roll of film. In her darkroom, she switches off the red light and removes the film from her camera. She winds the film onto the spool and drops it into the developing tank. She pours in the developer and screws on the lid. Later, after the film is taken out and dried, she makes a contact sheet and prints off several of the clearest images. She hangs them on the drying line. The photographs reveal sections of the woman's appearance: a face caught between pain and anger. She looks scared, Ana thinks. A woman ready for this charade to be over. On the last picture, Ana notices a smudge on the woman's finger. At first, she doesn't understand its significance. Then she looks closer—she can make out part of a ring. She dashes to the telephone stand in her hallway and calls her lovers to ask them both to come over straight away.

Upon arrival at her flat, Henrik says he will leave, while Grgur proposes they photograph their impending threesome. Ana ignores both suggestions and ushers the men into her darkroom. Grgur and Henrik loiter near the door, squinting in the blur of red light. Ana plucks the photograph from the drying line and props it against the headboard.

"I don't know whose wife this is," she says. "But I've had enough."

Grgur sits next to the print. A whitish nub, a burn welt, scars his cheek. "Maybe she will join us?"

"Unlikely," says Ana. "I broke her nose."

Henrik plays with the padlock on the door. "She's not my wife."

Grgur runs his hand over his slicked gray hair. "It doesn't matter who she is."

"She's married to one of you."

"Prove it," says Grgur.

"Give me your wallets," she says.

The men demur until Ana threatens to call their homes and speak to their wives. Both men pass their wallets over. Ana searches for pictures. Neither wallet has photographs, only state identification cards and a little money.

"Describe your wives to me."

Henrik glances up. He clutches Ana's photograph in his hands. "This woman looks more like you. An older version."

"Enough of the mind games," she says. "Answer me."

Grgur sticks his wallet back into his pocket. "My wife's thin, small-chested, older than me."

Henrik rolls the photograph up in his hands. She thinks he has understood the strategy behind Grgur's lies. "Mine's white-haired. Very old," he says.

"Perhaps the two of you are married to the same woman."

Before the men can contest that thought, Ana retreats to the kitchen and comes back with her bottle of rakija and two glasses. She pours the drinks on the nightstand. Most likely her lovers will continue their ruse of innocence. They do not trust her but stay in the darkroom for the possibility of sex. She signals to Grgur and Henrik that they can get drunk. The two men do not seem to hear her. They sit silently on the mattress, smoking. They face the full-length mirror— they stare into the silvered glass, entranced by the waterlike surface.

Ana leaves the darkroom and her flat, locking both men inside. She hurries to her old Fićo on the street outside.

Amber light from the lampposts illuminates little pockets of the road that she follows as she drives.

Sunlight breaks over the horizon as she cuts off the highway and passes through the outskirts of her hometown. Stone houses line the narrow streets, which curve serpentine around one another. She cruises up and down the steep roads, almost lost, her sense of direction faded for a reason she cannot place. Years have passed since her last visit— that timeframe she thinks is accurate. Her mind acts sleep-deprived, slow and sluggish, the spectral imprint of that woman in her dreams still interfering with her circadian rhythm. Henrik was right that the woman resembles her, but Ana never met her mother or knew what she looked like. Her father once confessed to Ana that her mother had run away. Institutionalized, she had always thought.

Ana heads to the cratered lake, a kilometer out of Imotski, and parks close to the ridge. Out of the car, Rolleiflex in hand, she makes her way to the lip of the crater. She stares down the side of the cliff into the dark water, considering what it takes to be one of the human birds who dive in during the summer, and also the jumpers who willfully plunge—once or twice a year—onto the rocks far below.

She kneels at the edge, lifts her camera, and peers through the viewfinder, the churn of water filling the frame. Her fingertip lingers over the shutter release. A cold wind blows around her, and she notices a lone pratincole swoop to the lake. She shoots a few pictures, the bird always out of frame. Somehow the Rolleiflex suddenly feels weightless, shorn from her grasp. The camera spins as it tumbles down, then strikes the rocks, scattering pieces of the plastic body and shards of lens into the water.

Ana considers the perilous drop—whether she would survive a fall, unlike so many. Whether it mattered to her if she did not. She straightens up, feels the wind and the cold, and backtracks to her Fićo. Inside, she cranks back the seat, lies stiff, her eyes closed. Sometime later, after a formless, empty sleep, she speeds away, unable to recall starting the engine. She slips by her father's cottage, stopping a distance down the road, letting the engine idle. The house is dark and uninhabited, her father's car absent from the driveway. It felt like a lifetime ago when she had sat next to her father's gravestone, trying to understand why he had refused to search for her mother. She had confessed a desire to see her mother again, to talk to her, ask her where she had been. Ana had shied away from admitting her affairs with older men or the incident with her young student. The little girl had claimed another's pencil drawing as her own and written her name below the sketch, a house with crude figures peering out from the windows. She had stolen another child's vision of a happy family. No one was allowed to do that.

Ana drives on, instinctively making her way to the school where she taught. The iron gates are open, the playground quiet. She parks behind the cars at the side of the main building. Waiting there, even for a minute, feels like a mistake, and she climbs out and goes into the school. The lobby is dark. She veers into one of the hallways. Square windows in each classroom door glow a clinical white. Ana peers through the glass panels, trying to remember the name of the girl. She had an old-fashioned name, like Dragica or Ljubica, but it was neither of those. Ana approaches the final classroom at the end of the hall. She pauses at the lit window.

Inside, a dozen children sit in a horseshoe arrangement of desks. Ana cannot see the girl she hit, even when she enters.

"Where is she?"

The teacher freezes by the blackboard. "Who are you?"

Ana does not recognize the woman—her replacement—and suspects the girl is hiding. Yet, as she glances around, the children remain unfamiliar to her, their pale faces blank. They watch her. Then they lower their eyes. The teacher shouts *policija* to a man in dirty gray coveralls at the door. Ana takes another look around the classroom—a strange pressure constricts her throat. She brushes past the janitor in the doorway and runs to the exit. Loud voices call out after her.

Once in her car, Ana avoids checking the rearview mirror. She drives out of the playground, past the gates, and through the red stoplight at the end of the street, barely even thinking to breathe as she finds the highway. The line of black asphalt stretches out to the horizon, back to Zagreb and her lovers in the darkroom. They could have easily forced the padlock, but she understands they crave her. They want to be captured. As the engine stutters, sounding out its death throes, Ana recalls her first camera, given to her many years ago by her father. The Altix had a receipt in the sleeve of its black leatherette case—the box camera had belonged to a woman named Marija Horvat. Ana often wondered what had happened to the woman and why she no longer owned the camera. At night, as a child, Ana stood in front of the mirror, focusing the lens of the Altix. Why had the woman let such a precious thing go?

Sojourn

Mateo, it is very late. Let me remember once more.

A few years after the war, I left Hrvatska without a word and started my life again in Norway. Even as I stepped onto the plane, I knew you would be unaware for some time of the circumstances surrounding my abrupt departure. At that moment, in the summer of 1999, I was fully ready to disappear into the blur of the new millennium. Yet it did not turn out like that: I was only a month away from meeting my future wife. Hanne was an administrator at the University of Bergen. She had a solid if unremarkable job, and our beige courtship seemed to satisfy her. Of course, during our first year together, it became clear she was ill-prepared to have a relationship with someone like me.

At that time, I had quit my teaching job in Zagreb, quit drinking, and, for a while at least, quit you. I am sorry I did not bring you with me to Oslo. In my brief period of enforced sobriety, I often considered our affair and your vulnerable state. The fact that I had never been with another man before and that you were half my age.

My favorite of our conversations was our first one in the café, when you changed out of your uniform in the restroom and returned in blue jeans and a striped wool sweater. Cologne glossed your neck. We sat at an outside table, our knees almost touching, my shoe tip abutting your sneaker. You drank espresso while I nursed a bottle of pilsner. You asked me to enlighten you about the books we were forbidden to teach in school.

"Mateo," I said. "You needn't call me Mr. Vitezić. It's

Toma."

You blushed. Still, you listened as I reeled off a list of writers. I enjoyed showing off for you. I taught you about the French poet Rimbaud, his short writing career, his affairs with older men, especially Verlaine.

Our weekly meetings intensified to after-school flirtations in the classroom, then in my quarters on the school grounds. I sneaked you in under the cover of night. You would not stub out your cigarette; you were hopeful the head of the school would spot you, force our relationship out in the open.

You kissed me first. Your lips were rough, the hair around your lips and chin soft and dark. You felt good, experienced. I suspected you had been with another man or one of the other boys. Perhaps Roko, Tomislav, or Petar. In my bedroom, I confessed all this was new to me.

"Never?" you said.

"In the HV there was someone."

You pressed me on the soldier's name. I told you nothing physical had happened and laughed and pulled away. I went to the galley kitchen and made us both a drink. I handed you a glass of rakija, and we sat quietly for a moment. We drank for courage and to see where it would take us. We had clumsy sex in the dark, over too quickly, and you slipped away in the early hours. Our relationship continued via these fleeting encounters in my quarters. I often asked you to stay the night, but you never did. I wondered if you were seeing someone else; I questioned you once directly. You rolled out of bed, threw on your shirt and jeans, and finally said no. At the end of the spring semester, when you graduated, I feared you would forget me. You had a scholarship to the University of Zagreb. A covey of young and old men alike would be around. You always said my jealousy would end us.

Before the faculty left for the summer, I received a summons from the head of the school for a disciplinary meeting. I knew this was the end for me. Sitting in his office, I half-listened to his lecture on the gulf between Catholic values and homosexuality. I barely cared now that you were gone. Within a few days I cleared out my quarters. In a dirty hotel room, I wrote you a goodbye note in a copy of Verlaine's *Sagesse*. But I did not know what address to mail it to, and I had no time to find it.

My brother had secured me a junior position at his advertising firm in Oslo, and I caught a flight, leaving you behind. It was clear, then and now, that the life of a literature teacher is ample preparation for the profitable misuse of our language. Croatian has little value in the rest of Europe. My near-fluent English and German were the reasons that I had any cultural or financial worth outside of the former Yugoslavia.

This was my first time out of the country, and I was unsure of how men treated other men there, especially ones who vacillated between men and women. Around the bars of Oslo, I drank and flirted with a handful of girls. But I could never take them back to my brother's flat. His wife already put up with so many of my bad habits. She demanded that I quit drinking and treating work like a joke. I tried to. A couple of weeks into my job, I traveled to Bergen on assignment from my brother. His brief noted something about reviving the blåskjell market, developing a campaign to get younger people into eating blue mussels. The company director, Herr Johannessen, was a stout silver-haired man of German descent. He wore an unbuttoned suit jacket, a checkered waistcoat underneath, a mismatched pair of trousers. He gave me a tour of the processing plant, then took me to his office where a spread of blåskjell sat in a chafing dish packed with ice. With a cocktail stick, I speared one of the slimy lumps of sea-meat and chewed it vigorously, almost choking on the brine. I offered Herr Johannessen my thoughts on pairing the delicacy with some type of strong alcohol, and he grinned and whisked me off to a cocktail bar in Nygårdshøyden, near the university. We drank several glasses of akvavit and looked through his book of ideas for publicity and his set of design drawings. I complimented Herr Johannessen on his sketches. "Please, Toma," he said. "Call me Lars." He admitted he didn't like the taste of shellfish, but what was he to do? His father had entrusted the plant to him, and it provided a good living. "I can meet many men this way," he said. He grazed my knee and though I was tempted to relive my experiences with you, I told him he had made a mistake.

Lars coughed a little, then removed two hundred kroner from his wallet and paid the bill. After he left, I ordered an orange juice and took from my briefcase a copy of Kundera's *The Unbearable Lightness of Being*. I read the opening page several times, unable to concentrate on the abstract philosophical language. I considered going after Lars. But I had caused him enough embarrassment. I closed the novel and rested my glass on top. I surveyed the room. A group of women were seated in the corner. I smiled at the tallest one. Her hair was cut in a bob, her face moonlike, boyish. She wore a dark blazer and white pants, and a chunky tortoiseshell pendant hung around her neck. When she came to the bar for a round of drinks, the bartender acknowledged her, revealed her name was Hanne. She glanced my way and quizzed me about my book.

I answered in my pidgin Norwegian. She cupped her ear, so I switched to English. "It's a slow read but I like it."

"I wish I had more time for books."

"I can read for you and offer pithy summaries."

She laughed. I removed my glass and slid the book along the counter. She examined the author's biography. "Are you Czech?" she asked.

"Close," I said. "Croatian."

My nationality silenced her for a moment. I could tell she had an urge to ask about the war, how it had affected me. What could I tell her about the rifle I'd never fired? Or the soldier I'd thought I loved? That part of my life was behind me. She straightened the beer mat in front of her and began to talk about her family, far north in Trondheim. She let slip that she had never left Norway, save one childhood trip to Sweden.

"This is a beautiful country," I said. "Why leave?"

"The cold. I'd like to feel the warmth of the South of France, perhaps visit the Italian coast."

"Italians vacation on the Croatian side of the Adriatic. We have the islands, the boats that sail down to Greece."

"That sounds wonderful."

"Perhaps I am overselling it," I said. "My homeland is a place of contradiction."

The bartender slid a trio of wineglasses across the counter. She glanced back at her friends. They waved for her to return to her seat. She scribbled her number on the beer mat. I took out my wallet and pressed my brother's business card on Hanne. "You can reach me here," I said. "My name is Toma."

It was Herr Johannessen who telephoned my brother first. Lars complained about my unprofessional conduct, my brusque Slavic manners. He said he would not use the company's services again. I assured my brother I would apologize to Lars and re-secure the contract. In truth, I wanted a second trip to Bergen to track down Hanne and discover why she had not called. I had an idea she sensed something different about me, beyond my foreignness, a dangerous, closed-off quality. I wasn't sure I liked that.

At the train station, I dialed Hanne's office and left a message with her colleague. "Tell her I'll be at the same bar tonight."

I caught a cab to the processing plant. Inside the lobby, the secretary said I should wait. An antique blueprint was tacked to the wall. The series of interlocking rectangles appeared to depict the plant.

Lars entered the lobby, smoking a cigarette. He beckoned me to follow him into his office. As I went in, he stayed near the door. He exhaled a long stream of smoke and watched me stand awkwardly by his desk. He came over and sat down, motioning for me to do the same. He stubbed out his cigarette in a large glass ashtray. "I would like you to apologize," he said.

"There was a misunderstanding," I said. "For that I'm sorry."

"That's not enough." He gathered the papers on his desk and flipped through them, reading some words under his breath.

"Goran appreciates your business," I said.

"Do you?"

"Of course."

"Then you must have a drink." He opened a drawer next to him and brought out a paper sack. He said it was a special drink, and he uncorked the bottle and swigged some down. Then he offered me the sacked bottle, and I took it and peeled back the brown paper. A black label bore the word Mjød in white script and a crude drawing of a Viking. I lifted the mead to my lips, a glob of his spittle hung on the lip. I closed my eyes and knocked back a large shot. The honeyed wine coated the back of my throat.

"Are you ready?" he asked.

"For?"

Of course, I knew. I was curious about this older man, the shape of his cock, whether he was cut. I came around to his side of the desk. I got to my knees and unbuttoned his fly. He spoke a few words of Norwegian, a phrase I could not work out. To my surprise, he was circumcised, yet his length of grayish skin looked sickly. I leaned in but he asked me to wait. He dipped his finger in the bottle and dabbed a few drops of mead on his tip. He winced a little, then he ran his fingers through my hair for me to begin. I shut my eyes and worked Lars for a while, and he apologized several times for his periods of limpness. When he finished, he stood and pulled up his trousers. "Send my best to your brother," he said.

I exited his office and took a taxi to the bar near the university. I ordered a glass of akvavit and carried it to the bathroom. I stood in front of the mirror and threw the drink back, swilling the spirit around my mouth, finally spitting it into the basin. I went back to the counter and asked for a second. The bartender inquired whether I was sick. "Yes," I replied, "but get me another."

I thought of you as I waited for Hanne. I had introduced you to rakija, to the pleasures of the fifth and sixth drink, that slow warmth that overtakes your body, makes you feel desired and attuned to the desires of your fellow man.

I had reached a perfect balance between these two states when Hanne came into the bar.

"I almost didn't come," she said.

"Because of your friends?"

"No. I don't know anything about you."

"You know I like books."

"True," she said.

I ordered two glasses of Bordeaux blanc. I tried to impress her with what I knew of the Sémillon grape, the type of soil it must grow in. She confessed she would just ask for white wine. I offered up some jargon—viticulture, terroir— and held my wineglass up to the light. She smiled and asked me to tell her something about my life. I told her I worked for my brother in Oslo, that I came to Bergen regularly for business. Hanne remained quiet, polite in the Norwegian way of doing things. She fooled with the top button of her blouse. I noticed she avoided eye contact and directed her gaze at the liquor bottles on the backbar. "Sorry," she said. "I had a long day. I'm not good company." She brought out her credit card from her bag.

"I have this," I said.

"You don't have to. But thank you."

I sipped my wine and considered how to lighten Hanne's mood. The cobblestones on the dark street outside shimmered in the glare of the white streetlight. "We should go for a walk."

"I don't do one-night stands," she said.

"That's not what I'm after."

"Good," she said. "Then we can go."

Hanne and I strolled around the city center, making our way toward the harbor. We paused in front of a line of moored fishing smacks. A chill wind blew in from the North Sea. We backtracked and huddled in the doorway of a Kaffebrenneriet. We sipped mugs of steaming cocoa and watched a fine mist settle over the town. I stayed at Hanne's place that night. We kissed a little on the sofa, then she said we should wait, and she retired to her bedroom. I waved her goodnight, but her door was already closed. I lay back on the sofa. I tried to forget about what had happened with Lars and instead picture Hanne naked, her narrow hips, her tangle of pubic hair, but my mental image of her would not materialize. I saw only you.

Though I was still living with my brother and his Norwegian wife in Oslo, I asked Hanne to visit me. I told her over the telephone she would have my room. She countered that she would stay in a hotel. "Fine," I said. "I just prefer to see you here."

Late Friday afternoon, after browsing several book stalls, I picked up Hanne from the train station and escorted her to a grand hotel one street over. She wore a sleeveless dress and had a cardigan folded over her arm. She said she was glad it was warm. She had me stay outside her room while she dropped off her bag. When she came out, she had on her cardigan, which flattered her more than I'd expected. A fresh, light pink gloss shone on her lips.

We walked to a local bistro and ate bowls of fårikål. I managed to shield much of my old life in Croatia, telling her little beyond a few details of my upbringing in a Communist-era tower block. Instead I steered the conversation to the work I did with my brother: the long hours of paperwork interspersed with spurts of developing creative slogans for food companies. Hanne smiled, seemingly impressed by my rise in social class. She drank more wine and probed how I spent my Sundays, then after my obfuscation, asked directly about my spiritual life. I sidelined her with a story about my first attempt at yoga, a sprained ankle after falling from the Trikonasana pose.

While we waited for dessert, I gave her a first edition of Kundera's novel. She clutched the book and examined the front of the dust jacket. The silver-gray cover bore a three-dimensional typeface. "Is he famous back home?"

"Yes," I said. "Sadly, the rest of Europe has barely heard of our famous writers, Danilo Kiš or Borislav Pekić."

Hanne laughed. "Sorry, I'm one of those people."

"You could borrow my copies, but they're in Zagreb."

"How long has it been since you've gone back?"

"A while."

"Why?" she said.

"My brother is here, my job."

"Advertising doesn't seem like your passion."

"Well, there's no money in reading."

That evening, I dropped Hanne back at her hotel and walked to my brother's in the gray of dusk. The next day I asked if she would like to drink at a hip cocktail lounge I had heard of, but she said she preferred to tour the cathedral.

I knew little about the Lutheran denomination. Hanne told me about High Mass and the order of the liturgy, about the vital Confession of Sin. As we stood outside, we heard the striking up of organ music. I pulled her away from the entrance. She resisted at first, then relished her hand in mine. We enjoyed a glass of red wine back at her hotel. I teased her over her skittishness and quizzed her about the last man she had dated.

Hanne fell silent. She had wanted to tell me, she said, about Espen, her failed engagement, the life she had almost led. He was gentle, unlike a soldier, had a mindset different from those of the Eastern Europeans. In anyone else's voice, I would have taken offense to those words. Hanne was earnest, painfully so, even when she said that she and Espen had broken up on poor terms. "It was my fault it didn't work out," she said. "I expected too much." She lifted her wineglass, holding it in midair. "Who did you leave behind in Croatia?"

"My students. I used to be a teacher."

"I thought you had that way about you. But there must have been someone."

"People come and go."

"That's a callous thing to say," she said.

"Perhaps I felt that way back then."

"And now?"

"And now I feel we should go to your room."

She replaced her wineglass on the coaster. "I don't want to do that."

"Hanne, did I say something wrong?"

"I understand you've been through a lot, but we don't know each other. And you haven't told me much about yourself."

"I'd like to change that."

"Perhaps next time we can talk more," she said. "I have to catch my train."

"I'll walk you back to the station."

"No. I know the way." Hanne picked up her bag, studied my face for a moment, then disappeared through the archway.

I stayed and finished the rest of the bottle. I thought over my suggestion to go to Hanne's room. I knew that she would not have said yes, that she might take offense, but something in me had to ask. Perhaps, in that moment, I was close to confessing my encounters with Lars, and the soldier, and you.

The bar eventually whittled down to a pair of businessmen in the corner. I watched them consume a great deal of Scotch and speak of the problems of the Vålerenga football team. I considered joining them, as I knew a little about the Eliteserien, but when I stood they eyed me, as certain men do, then looked away, uninterested. On my nightwalk home, I remembered how easy my love affair with you had been, the execution and escalation of our physical attraction. Things should have been simple in this open, embracing country, but for me they were not.

My brother's wife caught me entering the flat very late. I brushed past Linnea, went to the kitchen, and extricated a bottle of pilsner from the refrigerator. She stood in the doorway in her thick robe.

"You've already had enough."

"Just a nightcap," I said. "Do you or Goran want one?"

"He's asleep. I'm glad he doesn't see this."

"He knows me."

"We don't want you here anymore."

I uncapped the bottle and took a long swig. She turned around, skulked back to her bedroom.

I avoided Linnea as best I could for the next week. My brother never uttered a desire for me to find new lodgings, and I did not bring up the subject either. At work, he assigned me administrative tasks, mostly checking on the accounts of former clients, some of which went back ten years. I tackled my new clerical duties with superficial gusto, glad for the break from visiting Lars and Hanne.

In the evenings, I sat around in bars and drank heavily, then trolled a series of disreputable alleys for someone unknown to me, a man or woman ignorant of my past. These encounters always ended with the demand for kroner and my backing off, realizing what I was doing, the low I had come to. The final time I ventured out, two men jumped me, kicked me in the ribs and head, threatened to stab me if I didn't hand over my wallet. I saw no blade, but I gave them what money I had.

My time at work felt lengthened by my nighttime follies. My brother had noted my late returns to his flat, my decreased productivity on the accounts. At the end of the week, he marched into my office, a file in his hands.

"Linnea heard you last night," he said.

"Oh?"

"She said you were making a lot of noise."

"Goran, I was looking for a book."

My brother studied me, acutely aware of the way I was rubbing my forehead. "You look in pain."

"Just a headache."

He cupped his hand under my chin and lifted my head.

He studied the bruise on my cheek. "I can see why."

"It's nothing."

"Apologize to Linnea tonight." He placed the file in front of me. "Herr Johannessen wants to talk about the ad campaign."

"Again?"

He tapped the telephone on my desk. "Just call him."

"I'll find some time later."

"I mean it." He handed me the receiver and left my office. I knew my brother was holding in most of his anger. Of the two of us, he had been the quiet one, the diligent worker, a man later devoted to the selling of ideas. I could not hold it against him. I owed a debt to him and his wife.

I busied myself for the rest of the day. I flipped through the file a few minutes before five. I could taste the muscular coarseness of the blåskjell, and I pushed each number slowly, hoping the call would not connect. Lars answered almost instantaneously. "I'd like to run a new idea past you," he said.

"Sure," I said. "Go ahead."

"No, in person. I'd like to get your thoughts on my sketches."

His desperation felt transparent, and I imagined him in his office, a mass of nerves and back sweat, a thunderous erection under his desk.

My visit to Bergen surprised Hanne. She flitted around her living room, gathering up her clothes and a stack of magazines. When she had tidied the place to her satisfaction, she joined me on the sofa. Her face had reddened, her eyes wet. I asked if she was alright, and she leaned forward and kissed me, her aggression taking me by surprise. Then she lay back and drew up her skirt. She remained quiet during sex, her body limp, as though she had changed her mind. I whispered into her ear, asking if she wanted to stop. She said nothing. After it was over, she started to cry. She explained that she should not have slept with me. I held her. I told her she ought to move to Oslo and that we could move in together. As she broke away and left me on the sofa, she said I should ask her again in the morning.

In the late rush of us leaving her flat the next day, I pretended I had forgotten to ask. Hanne kissed me on the cheek as we parted ways at the intersection. I watched her catch the tram. I felt unsure whether she had really wanted me to bring up Oslo again. She was shy, rarely said what she desired, what she sought from me. She had not even mentioned the faded bruises on my body.

Before I left Bergen, I paid a visit to the processing plant. Lars was in the wash-up room scrubbing his nails. He wore a white lab coat and a hairnet. He stepped over to the roll of paper towels and dried his hands. Beneath the harsh light he seemed old, his face gray and wrinkled.

"It's been some time," he said.

"Goran has me working with some new clients."

"You moved on."

"That's one way to put it."

Lars approached, and I could smell on his clothes and in his hair the remains of iced salty fish. "Are you clean?"

"I've been traveling all day."

"That isn't what I meant," he said. "I know you've been with women."

"So?"

"I want you to appreciate me."

"Goran and I do."

"There are no sketches."

"I know."

"Then why did you come?"

I felt unable to answer Lars. We both knew why I was there: my attraction to men was something I could not repress in the right company. He kneeled before me and unzipped my trousers. I did not try to stop him. He unwrapped a condom and slid it on me. Then he took me in his mouth. I watched his bobbing hairnet. I could see his slick silver hair below the white net, the sweat gathering at the top of his scalp. When I had finished, he skinned off the condom, inspected the contents, then swaddled it in a paper towel and threw it away.

On my subsequent visits to stay with Hanne, I sought Lars out before I left Bergen. We would meet in his office. He would perform his mead ritual and say *Jeg ønsker å ha sex med deg*, which meant he wanted to have sex, though we never did. We took turns satisfying each other—twenty minutes at most and that would be it. My departures rarely provoked anything more than a few words, but Lars promised he would write me. I always turned away. Our encounters elicited little emotion from me, and I did not want to hear about his love for me or the sadness of his marriage. I was sure he was hiding a wife. After our last dalliance, he tried to kiss me, and I tasted the sourness of his breath. He asked if I would like to stay the night at his house. The flash of anguish in his voice struck me as dangerous. My future lay with Hanne. I decided I would not see him again.

A few months later, Hanne and I moved into a turn-of-the-century building in Grünerløkka, a gentrified district of Oslo. The main window of our flat faced the Akerselva River and an art gallery, once an old textile factory. Hanne sat in the little nook by the window and watched the visitors, the faux art trinkets they carted out. When she got tired of this, she took a job teaching ESL at a folkuniversitet. She rarely complained about the low pay or the difficult adult students. After work, I would meet her outside of the cathedral and we would walk the streets, look at the façades of the museums and galleries, continue on to the reptile park, stopping some days to listen to the roar from the feeding show. The cheers and claps of the crowd drowned out the alligators breaking bone and ripping flesh. We usually didn't stay for long but went for a coffee. She labeled our flâneuring her daily exercise, but I knew she was re-creating our first walk in Bergen. I asked her once and she looked at me strangely. "You seemed like a different person back then," she said.

That same day, we caught the tram home. Hanne took the one free seat, while I stood, clutching the handrail. Outside, buildings flitted by. Cars whipped past. The window of sky empty, just a pale patch of blue. As we approached the Tinghuset stop, I pointed across the road to an octagonal-shaped church. I told Hanne the central dome looked odd.

"What is that supposed to mean?"

"Not much. Just that it looks odd."

Hanne offered her seat to another man. She stood behind me. "How would you know? You're not from here."

I considered letting the matter lie. But something in her tone irritated me. "Maybe I should go back to Croatia."

I felt her hand at my back, pulling me around. "No," she

said.

"But I'm a different person." I did not say anything more. The tram rumbled over the bridge across the Akerselva River and pulled into Heimdalsgata. By this time, Hanne and I had turned away from each other. What I had said was hurtful and had upset our relationship's delicate equilibrium, but it was not in me to apologize. Once the tram juddered into motion, we began to argue again, this time over where to get married. She wanted it in the Lutheran cathedral, but I did not. I confided to her that I was a lapsed Catholic, for a host of reasons, and I could not abide any type of religious ceremony. She slipped her hand into my jacket pocket—a gesture, I thought, of acceptance— and I interlaced my fingers with hers. As we alighted from the tram, she reluctantly agreed to a civil ceremony. A few months later we married at City Hall. Her parents were in attendance, and a handful of her Bergen friends, and my brother and his wife. Leaving the room, walking past the colorful murals, Hanne told me she was happy.

Sometime later, Lars rang me at work. I said nothing about Hanne. "It's over," I said. He begged me to take one more trip to Bergen. I told Lars he was too old and hung up. For a long time afterward, it felt as though I had taken out my frustration with you on Lars. I tried very hard to forget about my past life. Hanne and I talked about children. We had a close call once, but lost her. I joked a Slavic-Nordic child would be an odd combination, and Hanne refused to talk to me for a week. We recovered mostly after that. We talked about other things: our careers, our holiday plans, a trip to Bergen to stay with her friends. I pretended to be sick the day of the trip, and she went without me, and I drank all evening with my brother.

Hanne ended our relationship the other day. She discovered a cache of letters from Lars. The silly old man had sent one every few weeks to my brother's flat, and his wife hadn't had the wherewithal to burn them. Perhaps in an act of longstanding resentment, she had sent them on in a brown paper package. That morning, Hanne had been sorting through some of my clothes in my suitcase for a vacation we were planning together, a sort of delayed honeymoon. When I returned home, she fanned the letters on the kitchen table, asked me to explain. I resisted at first, said the letters were a prank. Then an old man's fantasy. Finally, I admitted what the letters said was true.

Hanne screamed that I had betrayed her and demanded that I leave. I slipped away without saying anything else. I walked into town; I felt half there, a spectral presence in the midst of so many people. I stepped around the crowds and headed into an ornamental park. I studied the empty base of the ice rink and sat on the edge, feet dangling above a bed of red and brown leaves. A group of teenagers on the other side laughed at me, and I retraced my steps and bought a half-liter of brandy and drank it in the toilet of the Vinmonopolet. In the last hour of daylight, I stumbled back to my brother's flat. I slept in my old bedroom for several hours. In the morning, my body felt wretchedly cold. I told my brother that Hanne and I had had a fight and I was letting her cool off. My brother barely flinched. He must have sensed my lies and the depth of my hangover. He said, "Don't be late for work."

But I am late, many hours now. I am on a train to the

airport. I do not know where you live, all these years later. I hope I will still find you, Mateo. I have thought about what to say and if you would even listen. Before I left my brother's flat, I looked again for the book I meant to give you years ago. Though that copy of Verlaine's *Sagesse* is lost, left behind in a hotel room in Zagreb, I remember reading one of his poems to you, explaining that it was a confession. You pressed a finger to my lips and said no, it was an admission he had to return home.

Restoration

Aleksandar flew from Zagreb to Split trying not to picture his dying father in Chicago. For the entirety of the flight, he had refused to look out the window at the country of his birth. But in this moment the rolling land below fell away to the vast gleaming blue of the Adriatic. Out in the sea, scattershot islands lay off the coast. Tiny houses and churches lit up in a circus of reds and whites, and stands of juniper and olive trees sheathed the islands, fading out at the pebbled beaches. The airplane circled, descending through the turbulence to set its course onto the gray landing strip lined with winking lights. Aleksandar's motion sickness tore at his stomach and struck a dull ache in the back of his head. He couldn't imagine the ferocity of his father's lung cancer or the type of pain that required morphine. Years before, his mother had vanished during the civil war, and now he was on the verge of losing his father to disease.

As the airplane landed, Aleksandar pushed aside his guilt to focus on his second chance with Jana. It had been a year since they lived together in Zagreb. Their apartment had overlooked a patchwork of gardens, where stray cats hunted for mice in the undergrowth. Jana used to toss scraps to a rawboned tabby in the hopes of coaxing it to the balcony. The cat was too skittish for her to scoop up. Aleksandar was glad. He hated cats.

Part of him regretted their breakup, which had occurred for reasons he thought superficial. He was a decade older than Jana, though she rarely brought it up. During their last days as a couple, they had quarreled over money, over whether to move to a better part of Zagreb. Then at dinner they had argued, jokingly at first, about America's place in the world, then about Presidents Bush and Obama and the continued occupation of Afghanistan. Aleksandar demanded Jana cease ranting about colonizers and suggested that she just needed a beach vacation. He blamed her bad attitude on her youth. Jana accused him of being an overpaid banker, a jealous šupak, an American. Then she left the restaurant. Later that night, when she telephoned to say she wasn't coming back to the apartment, he spat all the dirty Croatian words he knew into the receiver until she hung up. She had her friends collect her drawing board and rolls of onionskin paper, her soapstone bowls full of rulers and architect's scales. They spurned his questions about where she was, what she was planning to do. Days later, when he learned of her relocation to Split, he had already slept with her friend Dorotea.

In the terminal, Aleksandar found Jana at the airport café. She was fiddling with a pack of cigarettes as she talked to the barista. She wore a light green shirtdress, which matched her painted fingernails, her blonde hair twisted into a topknot. He had forgotten the subtle touches she made to her appearance, the way they made him unsure. As his hand glanced her shoulder, he felt her sit straight up. Beyond surprise, he recognized doubt, even regret in her face. But he couldn't stop himself from handing her a birthday present. "Sorry it's late."

"You missed a great party."

"Something came up."

She tore off the colorful paper and examined the box. The gift was a distance meter, which he had purchased at a specialist store.

"It's state-of-the-art," he said. "It uses lasers."

"I know," she said. "Now let's go. I'm desperate for a cigarette."

Out in the parking lot, they climbed into Jana's Yugo. Without putting on her seatbelt, Jana started the ignition and sped the car up the service road, merging onto the highway.

Stickered along the bottom of the dashboard were postcards of the Croatian landscape. Aleksandar ran his finger across the picture of a bright blue pool of water. "Seems like you've been traveling."

"You always said I should." Her free hand dove into the center console and shook a cigarette from the pack and stuck it between her lips. She lit the end and waved away the cloud of gray smoke.

Aleksandar felt her answer was a half-truth, an attempt to mask her life without him. Her smoking was a private pleasure he couldn't share in. Or perhaps it was something else. He had always found her unfathomable, her motivations mysterious, selfish in execution. He wound down the window and rested his elbow on the doorframe. The road in front curved toward Split. The setting sun arced behind the belltower and cast a long shadow through the center of the old city. Undoubtedly the medieval buildings needed Jana's expertise as an architectural restorer. Yet, he knew from mutual friends that when she left Zagreb, she had become a preservation assistant, a demotion really.

"I was surprised by your e-mail," he said.

"It was my twenty-seventh birthday."

"A true milestone," he said. "So tell me about your new job."

"We're working on a church."

"Funny. You were never religious."

"One of life's ironies, I suppose."

"Perhaps. But how much do they pay you?"

Jana sucked harder on her cigarette and switched on the radio. "My life is fine."

Jana's apartment was in Radunica, near the vegetable market. Aleksandar had expected order and a keen sense of design, but inside, despite the high ceilings, the apartment felt cluttered and stank of burnt tobacco. On the floor sat a bulb-shaped terrarium full of cigarette butts and gray powdery ash. Against the wall was a tiger oak writing desk with brass claw feet. Drawings spread out across the tabletop, flanking a can of solvent and a plastic tray packed with shards of stone.

While Jana lingered near the archway to the kitchen, Aleksandar stood awkwardly by the sofa, feeling foolish that he had questioned her so aggressively. Before he had received her birthday party invitation, he had decided to return to the United States, to tend to his father in his final months. But her follow-up e-mail was so perfectly crafted it seduced him. She had called him Saša, like she used to, and she wrote of wanting to see him again, making a point that they had a lot of things to discuss.

"I'm sorry about before," he said.

"How about some champagne? It's left over from my birthday."

"Just seltzer and some aspirin."

"Stop being so uptight."

"Alright. I'll have a glass."

Her face softened, not quite a smile but something close. As she went into the kitchen, he noticed the bedsheet on the sofa, the blue fabric rumpled as though someone had already slept there. He smoothed the bedsheet with his hand, then smelled the faint scent of lemon detergent on his palm. He moved on to investigate the contents of the tray and thumbed dirt off a square of reddish stone. He heard Jana open the refrigerator, her rummaging through bottles and dishes, plastic bags of produce. When they had lived together, Jana had been a congenial host to his colleagues from Commerzbank. She would cook elaborate dinners and track down wines that would pair well. She often talked about her work transforming old municipal buildings into museums and galleries or the projects she wished to complete, the Romanesque basilicas and Gothic churches. In moments of self-doubt, she rubbed her bottom lip and ceded the conversation to Aleksandar—though his staccato remarks usually stayed with what little he remembered of Croatia's history. He missed her translating for him when he misspoke, the way her mouth correctly formed his words or retold his silly jokes.

Jana emerged clutching two wineglasses. She had removed the tie from her topknot and her hair now rested on her shoulders. She passed him a glass. "You've found one of my projects."

"Looks old."

"Yes," she said. "Roman tesserae from the palace."

He set the piece down carefully. "Well, it appears we're celebrating."

"A reunion."

He raised his glass and clinked it with hers. They sipped their champagne. His wine tasted flat and sugary, but if he complained she would accuse him of "Saša being Saša"— self-centered and always ready to play contrarian. In the past, Jana had charged Aleksandar of being an emotionless man, a ghost. He had confided very little in Jana, and he knew he could often be distant, uninvolved, impervious to those around him. His old therapist in the US had blamed the disappearance of his mother. After she vanished, a few days into the war, Aleksandar had fled with his father to America. Then he had become part of the post-millennium wave returning to the homeland, once it was safe. He had found few Croats would talk about the brutal events of the war, especially in public, and neither he nor Jana would bring up the trauma so many went through.

Birthday cards sat on the mantelpiece, and he cased the room for other signs she had entertained at her apartment. The bookcase held empty wine bottles and gift bags spilling over with crumpled wrapping paper. Against the radiator leaned her drawing board, its face dotted with yellow sticky notes. Some notes had names or good-luck messages. One sported a heart with *27!* in the center.

Jana sat on the windowsill. "It's strange having you here."

"I'm glad I came," he said. "So many things have been on my mind."

"I'm seeing someone."

Her admission didn't make sense to Aleksandar. He hadn't heard mention of a new boyfriend or lover from their circle of friends. Maybe she had kept the man a secret from everyone. Of course, this man would be a young Croat: taller and sensitive and more interested in her work than

Aleksandar ever was. Maybe this Croat was an architect or a doctor or worked with children and in his spare time painted picturesque watercolors of the Roman ruins. Maybe this Croat owned a cat.

"Why did you want me to come?"

"I thought we could take a trip," she said. "The islands are empty this time of year."

He looked again at the sticky notes for men's names: Teo, Stjepan, Luka. He was wary of who they were, of her words, her habit of changing the subject. And beyond that, he knew when she said *empty* she meant of tourists, primarily Americans. She meant the sightseers who did not really want to think about the war. She meant him.

"You were going to show me Split," he said.

"The islands are better," she replied, "and I can show you the Blue Grotto."

"Does your lover know about this?"

"Of course not."

"Is he around?"

Jana cradled her glass below her chest. "He's away for work."

"This feels like a mistake," he said. "I should have flown to Chicago."

"Why?"

"It's not important." In truth, he wanted to tell her about his father's illness, but he feared she would immediately send him away to look after his father. He knew for them to get back together—and for her to ditch this other man—she would have to see the good in him once again. Confessing to his night with Dorotea was out of the question. "A trip," he said. "Let's do it."

In the morning, they walked down to the ferry docks. Aleksandar, groggy after a poor night's sleep on the sofa, carried both their suitcases. After the champagne there hadn't been any serious talk—little beyond the news they would be staying at her friend's guesthouse. He had watched television to help drift off, but he had stayed awake thinking of the nurse inserting a cannula into his father's arm, before connecting the tube to an IV bag of morphine. Aleksandar knew his father's once-sharp mind would be dulled. His father, he imagined, called out for Aleksandar to sit at his bedside. He could be there, perhaps with Jana. But she would never go to America—she had a new relationship, didn't she? In this fit of doubt he had rifled through her desk drawers, then, finding just mechanical pencils and loose drafting dots, sat on the sofa and toyed with the distance meter, firing off the laser to measure the space between himself and Jana's bedroom.

Along the promenade, they stopped at Diocletian's Palace. Bullet holes cracked the marble of the peristyle in elaborate patterns. Jana surprised Aleksandar by talking of the wartime shelling, the frigate that terrorized the city. In his mind Aleksandar replayed the video he had seen of the attacks, the strafing rounds slicing through concrete and bone. The move to America with his father had come at the start of Yugoslavia's descent into civil war. At the time, and for a good while after, he felt guilty they had failed to find his mother and instead made a life for themselves in Chicago. In the intervening years, he often speculated on who he would have been if they had stayed behind. If he had lived in Croatia his whole life, he was sure Jana would judge him differently, if at all. For whatever reason, over the last couple of years, she had become his vital connection to his homeland, to proving he belonged here.

Aleksandar and Jana bought tickets for the ferry to Vis. On board the ship they hurried to the top passenger deck to take photographs of Split. The gray buildings of the naval base down the coast were barely discernable. Aleksandar took a shot of a missile boat and then deleted the out-of-focus image from his camera. The rest of his pictures were blurry, and he gave up once the ferry got under way. The roar of the engines filled the air, and the propellers churned the water, leaving a foam wake curving back to where they had begun. Soon the city flattened out into a disc on the horizon. Aleksandar's legs felt weak. He clutched the guardrail and breathed in the brisk air. The azure water darkened as the ferry powered farther out to sea. He shielded his eyes against the glare of the overhead sun. Jana sat in the shade of the funnel.

"Look for where we are going," she said.

"I prefer the coast. The line between land and sea."

"When did you become a philosopher?"

"Who knows?" he said. "I've always loved how the land falls away."

Jana came to the guardrail. She placed her hands on his shoulders and directed him. "Look that way."

"Fine," he said. A string of islands lay on the horizon. Here and there he could make out white yacht sails billowing in the wind. "What am I meant to see?"

"Everything."

"It's pretty," he said. "I love it."

"You keep using that word," she said. "Love love love love

love love *love.*"

"I say it to you when you're asleep."

"Funny," she said. "Real funny."

In the late afternoon the ferry sailed into port. They caught a bus to Komiža with a host of sightseers and day-trippers heading home. The bus weaved through vineyards and groves of olive trees, and Aleksandar marveled at the surrounding hills starred with pine and holm oak. On the highest peak was a stone chapel. Jana sat up in her seat and pressed her finger against the glass. She explained the chapel was dangerous to visit because of the old landmines. "The military kept the island off-limits until the eighties," she said. "And there are caves across the island. Tito commanded his forces from one during the Second World War."

The guesthouse turned out to be a tiny studio tucked behind a bakery, a short walk from the public beach. While Jana stopped at the kiosk downstairs for cigarettes, Aleksandar dropped the suitcases inside the door and poked around the apartment. Whitewashed walls and a long pine bookcase connected the small living room to the bedroom. Behind a frayed curtain was a galley kitchen, with postcards of cathedrals and churches taped to the refrigerator door. Aleksandar drifted into the bedroom section. In the corner stood a bulky television set topped with a dusty portrait of Marshal Tito.

Jana entered the studio clutching her cigarettes and a bottle of suntan lotion. She pressed the bottle into his hand and went to the closet. He sat on the edge of the mattress and raised his eyes to the ceiling. Brown water stains appeared perilously close to the bare light bulb. "I'm glad this apartment was free."

Jana opened the closet to a rack of men's shirts. "It's quirky," she said. "Of the Communist grandmother period."

"Evidently a randy grandmother," he said, pointing to a condom wrapper on the nightstand.

Jana grimaced and ran to the bathroom.

Aleksandar went to the glass doors, which led to a balcony and a paved terrace—where a ginger cat dozed on the sunlit tiles. He rapped the plastic bottle on the glass, but the cat yawned and scratched itself. Aleksandar drew the shades.

Jana came back with a large wad of pink tissue paper and crudely packaged the condom wrapper. "I'm taking a shower," she said.

"Good call." He retrieved his suitcase and slotted it between the closet and desk, unwilling to let his clothes encounter the general filth. He curled up on the bed, curious to see if she would join him afterward. He listened to the sound of the running water, the droplets striking her body and washing away the soap lather, but the noise became an indistinguishable pitter-patter, then nothing as he fell asleep.

When Aleksandar woke, Jana was at the desk typing at her computer. Blue light from the screen bled into the darkness of the room.

"What are you doing?" he said.

"Just catching up on some work. An idea for the church."

"No e-mails to your other exes?"

Jana swiveled around in the chair. "Don't be jealous," she said. "It's the worst thing about you."

"Thanks for telling me."

"I've told you plenty of times. You just never listen."

It irritated Aleksandar when she was like this. Her internal pendulum swinging to her combative side reminded him of the last weeks of their relationship, her stock criticism that he was prone to bouts of jealousy while the rest of the time he was switched off to the world. Her invective, brutal sounding in the Croatian language, had been one reason he had so quickly slept with Dorotea.

He surveyed the room. His suitcase lay open on the dresser. His shirts were hanging in the closet. She had also set up a cot in front of the nightstand. The canvas and metal pole construction didn't appear comfortable. Nor did the thin sheet and pillow.

"There's room here for both of us," he said.

"I presumed you'd take the cot."

"We slept together for a year."

"And look at where it got us." She closed the lid of her laptop. "Now are you taking the cot? Or am I?"

Aleksandar rolled to the edge of the bed. Perversely, he was enjoying this moment of Jana's attention and he unbuttoned his shirt, making sure to suck in his belly as he draped his shirt over the television set. He sprawled on the cot, pulling the sheet up to his chest. He watched her undress in the dim light. She slipped beneath the sheets naked. "Can you stop watching me?" she said. Just as he was about to object, he saw that she was already facing the wall.

A warm breeze blew as Aleksandar and Jana ate breakfast on the terrace. They devoured cheese bureks from the bakery and drank several cups of coffee. As they cleared away the dishes, Jana said it was time for that beach vacation he had always talked about. "We could both relax," she said. Aleksandar took her words in good faith, hopeful they could put last night behind them. She packed a lunch while he grabbed a paperback from the bookcase and one of the postcards stuck to the front of the refrigerator. They set off through the maze of streets and wound over to the hills. They took the dirt path through the scrub, where the dry earth smelled of pine needles. It was a sweaty, awkward climb, and Aleksandar's back hurt from sleeping on the cot. Jana stayed ahead of him. She wore shorts and a breezy yellow T-shirt, her feet snug in a pair of men's hiking boots she had found in the guesthouse. She glanced back now and again, waving for him to walk faster.

From the summit they could see the cove below. A thin band of shingle made up a pebbled beach. Parasols dotted the area and towels were laid out like colorful strips of paper. Several sunbathing couples had mesh bags bulging with bottles of red wine and loaves of bread and rectangles of cheese wrapped in wax paper.

As they made their way down the steps, they saw nude swimmers emerge from the surf. The men had potbellies and bronzed skin and small wrinkled penises. Many of them, Aleksandar suspected, were single Germans. They carried *Der Spiegel* as they roamed the beach or had thick political tomes poking out of their satchels. They had towels perfectly squared. In his experience, singledom and nudity went together. It was as if each of the men were saying: *This is who I am; this is what I have to offer.*

"I'm too old for this."

"It's natural," she said. "Our bodies are meant to be free." She lay two green bath towels in the shade of a carob tree. Then she stripped to her panties and rubbed suntan lotion across her shoulders and chest. Above her hip was a new tattoo, a dark indigo shape resembling a wishbone: a map of

Croatia. He was envious of her display of national pride, but more jealous that a man had touched her. One of the spots where she loved to be kissed. Without a second thought she peeled off her underwear and stuffed it into her bag. "Your turn," she said.

"Some of us are more modest."

"Ack!" she said. "Pay more attention to your Slavic roots."

Aleksandar shifted onto his side, as if he hadn't heard her. Though he wanted to look at her as she sunbathed, her admonition turned him off. He tried to settle in with his book, suffering through the novel's old dialect, skipping over so many words the plot unraveled. The story was set some time ago when Yugoslavia was whole—that much he grasped. Growing up in Rogers Park, Aleksandar seldom heard his father discuss the war or speak in his native language. His father said he was American. He loved greasy hamburgers and *Jeopardy!* and the vastness of Marshall Field's. He worked for years in a laundromat and was thankful for the clean, powdery air and the Cubs games on the television. But sometimes he brought up their vacations to Opatija, truncated memories of visits to the Benedictine abbey or anecdotes about the swimming lessons he gave Aleksandar in the shallows. His father's face paled when Aleksandar asked why they had fled the country and why they changed their last name from Čabrajec to Chabries. Only then did Aleksandar learn about the ethnic cleansing and that his mother had probably been one of the victims.

He marked his page with the postcard, then slid the book under the towel. He concentrated his energy on the sea and the waves crashing against the large black rocks jutting from the water. A group of naked teenagers paraded across the far side of the beach. A dreadlocked boy gawked at Jana's crotch. The boy lingered, pretending to talk on his cellphone, then he joined his friends.

Aleksandar nudged Jana's thigh. "That kid was leering."

She glanced over and let out a laugh. "The sun is getting to you," she said. "Time for a swim."

Aleksandar had never become a strong swimmer. He paddled and splashed around like a child. "Let's stay here."

Jana brushed sand from around her navel. Her skin gleamed from the oily suntan lotion. The boys peeked and took Jana's picture.

"I'm going to break his camera," said Aleksandar.

"They're kids."

"Perverts."

"Really, Aleksandar," she said. "Now, come on, the water's beautiful. We won't go too deep."

He followed her down to the shoreline, the foaming breakers streaming over his toes. She linked fingers with his, and they stepped into the shallows. The blue began to envelop their bodies. Jana said she loved how the water made her feel. She broke free from his grasp and waded out until the water reached her shoulders. As he joined her, he set his sights on the horizon, the flecks of gray that must have been far-off islands. He swam around her, drawn to her breasts.

Jana splashed water in his face. "You left your modesty on the beach."

"The salt is hurting my eyes."

"I haven't heard that excuse before." She floated on her back and bubbled seawater between her lips. "Are you naked yet?"

"If you quit pestering me." He plunged his hands down to

untie his drawstring. He held the shorts up as proof.

"At last," she said, looking over. She kicked forward and grabbed the shorts and pitched them toward the rocks. They landed off to the side and floated on the surface like a dead jellyfish. Then the current swirled the shorts beyond his sure footing.

"I didn't like that pair," he said.

When they returned to the apartment, they showered separately. Then they went for dinner at a seafood restaurant overlooking the bay. They drank and talked like old times. It pleased Aleksandar that Jana hadn't mentioned her lover since Split. Her affair with this man, or whatever it was, must now be over. He poured her another glass of wine and reminisced about their long strolls through Zagreb. Jana's face lit up. "We must have seen the entire city," she said. "Every church and cathedral." After Jana had left for Split, he had retraced their steps, attempting to work out how their relationship had vanished in the city around them. Now, over dessert, Jana teased him about wearing the towel like a skirt. She wondered aloud if he would have walked back naked. "Just to scare the Germans," he said.

Back at the guesthouse, they took turns stripping in the bathroom. They lay on top of the bedsheet in their underwear, letting the ceiling fan whirl air over their bodies. He knew she found him attractive—she had admitted once that his good looks were his best quality. He considered making a move, but hot pinpricks stabbed at his legs. He sat up to take a look: his thighs were pocked with tiny red circles. "This is why I hate cats."

She kneeled next to his calves, drawing a finger from

point to point. "They're fleabites," she said. "They come with the territory." She hurried to the bathroom and rummaged through the medicine cabinet. She returned with a tube of calamine and squeezed some onto her palm. She rubbed the lotion onto his legs. It reminded him of their old routine. The backrubs that quickly led to sex. He took her arm and pulled her down, the two of them now face-to-face, so close he could see the flecks of gray and yellow in her irises.

"It wouldn't be right," she said.

"I thought because of earlier."

"We have a lot to discuss."

"That's why I'm here."

Jana rolled off his chest. "I wasn't sure you'd come. After all, we've hardly spoken."

"Actually, not at all."

"Let's forget about talking," she said, "and just lie together."

Aleksandar knew she was delaying, but he didn't have much of a choice. He mirrored the curve of her body and cast his arm over her waist. He studied her nape, wanting to kiss a single spot of her buttery tan. Glorious freckles stippled her shoulders, her collarbone, the top of her chest. "Get the light," she said. He switched off the lamp and settled back at her side. His breath rustled her loose hair. She emitted a muffled grunt before craning her neck to kiss him. Her hips gyrated against him. She slid his hand into her panties and asked him to pull her hair and call her Dorotea. He tried to see if her eyes were open, but it was too dark.

At breakfast on the terrace Jana skirted Aleksandar's questions. She played with her sunglasses, folding the plastic arms in and out, and offered broad statements and answers that weren't answers. He pressed Jana on her vague responses, searching for evidence of her real feelings. In the night, after she had spat Dorotea's name, she had shifted to the side of the bed and not said another word. He had lain awake, wondering how long she had known. She seemed to have relished invoking her friend's name and denying him sex.

Jana whispered to the cat skulking past the table and it circled back and brushed its body against her legs. She put on her sunglasses and looked past Aleksandar, out to the islands. The cat mewed. Aleksandar growled to scare the cat away, trying not to catch his reflection in Jana's sunglasses.

He opened the novel he had started on the beach and removed the postcard. The image on the front depicted a Gothic church—a very familiar one: St. Mark's in Zagreb. A block of dense handwriting filled the back. He read a few words but became irritated by Jana's blowing of kisses at the cat. He flipped the postcard around and pointed to a strange-looking word. "Jana," he snapped. "What does this mean?"

She plucked a chunk of smoked salmon from her plate and dropped it next to the cat. "How do you barely know the language?"

"Don't feed him."

"Why not?"

"Who cares if I don't know the language?" he said. "Is this about last night? About Dorotea?"

Jana picked up the cat and settled him in her lap. She stroked his head and his ginger fur and the length of his wiggling tail. "You should consider why you're here."

"For you."

"Not *here*, but in the country."

"I don't know anymore," he said. "It doesn't matter. I'll have to go back to care for my father."

"Šime?" she said. "Is it serious?"

Aleksandar's heart warmed to her use of his father's Croat name. In Chicago, his father was known as Simon. "Yes. He's very ill."

"I'm sorry, Saša," she said.

"Is it callous that I came here first? That I had a vacation while he suffers?"

"Don't be so hard on yourself."

"I'm thinking when I return from Chicago, we could give it another go."

"I'm in a relationship."

"You said it wasn't serious."

"No, I didn't. Andrej will be back."

Aleksandar fingered the postcard and creased over the corners. "Just tell me this is about Dorotea."

"No," she said. "This is about my life and my decisions."

He lowered his eyes to the back of the postcard. As he stared at the words, he realized it was Jana's handwriting. He came around to her side of the table, holding the postcard in front of her. "This is your lover's guesthouse, isn't it?"

Jana snagged the postcard and smoothed it out on the tabletop. "Yes, but he also comes here with someone else. I don't know her name."

"So where does that leave us?"

"I don't know."

"That's all you have to say?"

"I hired a boat while you were sleeping."

He turned away and slunk through the doorway. "Get your money back or don't. It's your life." He flung his suitcase onto the bed and gathered his clothes from the closet and chest of drawers. He kicked the cot over and collected his wash bag from the nightstand.

Jana stepped into the room and slid the glass door shut. Her sunglasses were now in her hand. "Andrej doesn't know I'm here."

Aleksandar closed the lid of his suitcase. "I should have gone straight to Chicago."

"You'll see Šime soon," she said.

"My father had no doubts in leaving this country."

"He did what was right for you both."

"So many people here think he abandoned my mother."

"Croatia is changing," she said. "Rethinking its past." She reached out and touched his hand. "Listen, the boat is going to Biševo. We can visit the Blue Grotto."

The captain was waiting at the wharf. He was sitting in a deckchair, wearing a salt-stained Guayabera shirt and cargo shorts. In his lap lay a transistor radio. Samba music sailed out, light and tinny. He greeted Jana with a salacious grin, which departed his boyish face when he saw Aleksandar.

"Dobro jutro," she said.

"Da." He stood and folded his chair, then shouted to the two men on the deck. "Vrijeme je za posao."

Aleksandar had a rough idea of what the captain said, something concerning work. He listened in, slowly translating the words of the men. He almost laughed when the captain declared that Modra Špilja was for tourists. He didn't want to feel once more like an outsider in his own country. Even if Jana implied this was always the case.

The grizzled first mate leaped onto the wharf and untied

the mooring line from the bollard. He grinned at Aleksandar and stuck up his thumb.

"Da," said Aleksandar. "I am ready."

The fishing boat puttered out of the bay and into the open water frothing with large whitecaps. Aleksandar and Jana stood at the bow rail, a foot of clear space between them. Aleksandar saw the men were drinking rakija. They shot glances at Jana and muttered slurs, but she ignored them. She talked of a letter she would write Šime, the catalog of past events she wanted to ask him about: his life in America; the intimate moments he missed sharing with his wife; the raising of little Aleksandar. She knew Šime from photographs—his salt-and-pepper beard, the troubled smile betrayed by his eyes. She had always wished to meet him, she said. The father of Aleksandar.

Jana rested her head on Aleksandar's shoulder. He liked her weight against his body, the soft rise and fall of her chest, the feeling that she was warming to him again. If she gave him a second chance, he would be different this time, less of a ghost. They could live in Zagreb, in their old apartment. They could talk openly about his mother, all those who died. Maybe he would even fly in his father to see out the remainder of his life in his homeland.

Miles out, the swell grew. The captain sank another swig, his hips gyrating to the samba music. His crew laughed. They offered Aleksandar the bottle of rakija. He waved to say *no*; he felt light-headed. With his hands on the bow rail, he pushed out his feet to lower his center of gravity, then glanced up to a cirrus cloud, the only one in the sky.

Jana caressed the small of his back, rubbing her fingers

in tiny circles. "It's a natural remedy," she said. "You have a pressure point right there." She pressed harder, her nails digging into his skin. "Does that hurt?"

Aleksandar bowed his head and stared blankly at the water—relieved he could feel something. "No. Just right."

Her hand fell away. "That should hold you over."

"I should be braver," he said. "More like Andrej."

"You don't want to be like him. He's just a man of words."

"And of loose women."

She slapped his arm. "Your sense of humor will get you into trouble one day."

"Will it get us together again?"

"I haven't decided yet."

They fell silent for a moment. A flock of gulls squawked above the boat. Aleksandar eyed the parabola of their course, the warm currents lifting the birds up and toward the island. Golden light gilded the rocky coast and contrasted against the hills above, thick with dark pine. The boat headed for a sandy bay, where a rickety wooden dock stood and a group of tourists milled around a tin hut talking and laughing and taking pictures of the nesting gannets on a nearby skerry. As the boat skirted the shore, the crew stirred as if rising out of a stupor. The captain anchored the boat in the shallows, and Aleksandar and Jana jumped into the water and waded to the beach. They joined the line of people waiting on the dock.

Aleksandar was reluctant to appear as just another sightseer, but each time a rowboat came into view he felt a rush of anticipation. Bronze swirls decorated the prows, mirroring the wakes that churned around the dock's pilings. Jana talked excitedly with another couple about what lay ahead, but Aleksandar remained silent, skeptical of what this day would bring. When a boatman whistled to Aleksandar and Jana, they climbed down the ladder into the rowboat, and Aleksandar gruffly handed the man twenty kuna. The boatman had a substantial paunch, but broad shoulders and sinewy arms. He wore a shirt with faded chevrons on the sleeves and had an unlit cigar in his mouth. He rowed them past the skerry and around the tapering headland, where water purled against the striated rock. Spray hit Aleksandar's face. The salt in the air smelled primeval, and his desire to see the famous grotto grew. Around a spike of limestone they reached a narrow aperture in the cliffside.

The boatman spoke in a gravelly voice. Jana translated—"This was Tito's favorite cave..."—as the boatman spat his ruined cigar into the water and laughed. Aleksandar didn't get the joke but understood they were waiting for the waves to be right, so they wouldn't smash into the sharp overhang of rock. In silence, he watched the boatman, the knotted veins in his wrists, crisscrossing up to his thick knuckles. He held the rowboat steady as eddies swirled and crested against the hull. A burst of energy overtook him, and he heaved the oars with three great strokes. They ducked as the rowboat entered the cave. Consumed by the dark, Aleksandar felt a tightness in his diaphragm as though he had forgotten to breathe.

Light sparked somewhere deep in the cave. The boatman rowed them through the narrow channel—the towering limestone on either side darkened by olive-gray lichen. Then the boatman drew the oars from the water and crossed them. Droplets ran off the blades like miniature waterfalls. He stood and scraped a hooked metal pole against the cave wall, guiding the boat through. The cave opened up to a large glittering pool. Flaring light came from below, turning the water the oddest color: a radiant ultramarine.

Aleksandar let his hand trail in the pool. It felt cold, pure, like meltwater. The boatman said something in a low voice. Aleksandar couldn't translate the words. Jana whispered into his ear: "He says to keep your hands inside the boat. The rocks are very sharp."

"I've never seen anything like it."

"Sunlight reflects off the sand," she said. "There's a hole down there." She lifted her bag to her lap and pulled out the distance meter. "I thought we could try it out."

She pressed the meter to her chest before passing it to Aleksandar. He fiddled with the buttons until a laser pulsed across the cave. The red beam of light looked out of place amid the show of electrifying blues. He leaned over the side of the boat, holding the meter over the water. He bowed his head, listening to Jana's instructions, but he became distracted by the boatman's laugh. The meter slipped between his fingers, vanishing into the depths of the pool. He stood and lifted one foot onto the gunwale.

"Saša," she said. "What are you doing?"

Aleksandar dove clumsily into the pool. His forearms hit the water first, then his head. Through blurred vision he saw the meter sinking fast. He scissor-kicked his legs over and over, the burning sensation in his muscles tempered by the freezing water. Far out of his reach the meter hit the seafloor, sending up a small cloud of silvery sand. His body balled up, and he flipped around to swim up, but his strength felt sapped, and the pressure of the water pushed against his lips. The dark outline of the rowboat above shrank and rippled. As it dawned on him that he was drowning, a powerful force grabbed his shirt collar, and he felt his body changing direction, rising toward the surface, where he burst through and gulped the air, sputtering. In front of him the boatman was treading water, his reddened face inches from Aleksandar's. Jana held out the metal pole and Aleksandar pulled himself to the boat.

"You fool," she said. "Have you gone crazy?" She grabbed his wrist and helped him over the side. He lay splayed on the bottom boards like an exhausted fish. After a few seconds he sat up and brought his knees to his chest. She rubbed his back. Warmth radiated across his shoulders. His breathing slowed.

"You had me worried," she said.

"I thought I could get it."

"I don't know what to do about you."

"Maybe we could hide out here for a while?"

Jana seemed about to answer when the rowboat canted—the boatman was clambering in, grunting and cursing. His shirt had unfastened, revealing the wide expanse of his chest and the medal hanging from a silver necklace. He yelled at Aleksandar and spat at his feet.

Jana fished around in her bag and brought out a handful of bills. "Uzmi novac," she said.

The boatman waved the money away and drew the oars together. He rowed the boat through the channel to the curve of white light. Sooner than Aleksandar thought possible, they were out of the grotto and dealing with the growing swells of the sea. The brightness of the day surprised him, and his eyes took a moment to adjust. In the distance the other rowboats were heading toward the dock. The wind had picked up and was pushing the boats close to an outcrop of large black rocks. The boats bobbed wildly, while the men and women on board held one another, misted in spindrift.

The boatman steered the rowboat away from the cliffside, plotting a route back that took them farther into open water. Before long whitecaps pounded the prow and splashed over into the boat, pooling around Aleksandar's shoes. Jana slumped forward, her arms crossed and squashed into her thighs. Her gaze fixed on the boatman. He had started to talk in long swooping sentences, raising his voice as he repeated the same phrase over and over. Far above the boat airplanes roared across the sky, the jet engines masking the boatman's words. Aleksandar looked up at the sparkling contrails. Two lines of vapor diagonally crossed two more. He wished he were back at home in Chicago talking with his father. As he closed his eyes, the deep voice of the boatman reasserted itself over the distant rumble. Aleksandar wasn't sure what the boatman was saying until he recognized one of the words, then he could decipher the booming invocation: *Return. Return to the land.*

May Our Ghosts Stay With Us

In the winter of 1991 my grandfather's charred body appeared on the television news. The reporter lifted a blanket off my grandfather's face. His eyes had been hacked out with a knife and then his clothes doused with gasoline and set alight, and he was left to burn to death in the street outside of his house. I cannot imagine, even as I watch the newsreel again in the comfort of my university office, the pain he experienced. Or the shock my grandmother felt as the men made her watch. These men were not soldiers of the Yugoslav National Army or any official military. They were hired thugs and fanatics persuaded to cross the border and terrorize the villagers of Voćin.

For the last twenty years I have been processing the images of my grandfather's death. Aided by Xanax and a fine collection of Speyside and Islay whiskies, I have in recent months been completing his autobiography—ghostwriting the last part of his life.

I came across his diary in the papers of my father. Just after the millennium he died of a heart attack, and my mother shipped all his files to me. I hid the boxes in the corner of my office and draped the Croatian flag over them, trying to forget what lay beneath. After a decade of lecturing at the University of Zagreb, my career in the world of film studies had arrived at an impasse. I cared little about my students' thoughts on the metaphysics of Disney villains or the myopic post-everything theories of my colleagues. In truth, I felt a certain longing to be close to my father again, and I lifted off the flag, folding it neatly on my desk. Dust motes swirled in the air, catching the light. I watched the particles for a moment, then I sliced open the boxes, unearthing an archive of my father's life: folders of medical records, stacks of maps and weather reports, yellowed telephone directories, photographs of burned-out houses, six drafts of my father's sub-Brechtian play, each revision more misguided than the last. Stuck between a pair of historical volumes on Yugoslavia sat the diary: a plain leather-bound book.

I sequestered myself that whole afternoon and evening to read my father's thoughts. Yet something felt askew on the opening page—a litany of prayer titles: variants of "Oče naš," over and over. My father had always professed his agnosticism, and it was then I realized the diary was my grandfather's. I skimmed the rapturous veneration of the Trinity, glad when references to my grandfather's Catholicism disappeared. Rain poured outside as I continued to read, and I glanced out the window now and again to remind myself of the physical world. The chronicles of my grandfather's daily life became abstract and fragmentary; he preferred lists of Communist Party members and Latin bird names and snatches of overheard dialogue to anything cogent or meaningful. Life in Voćin seemed limited, parochial. Perhaps this was the reason my parents had never taken me to visit as a child. In retrospect, we had little contact with that side of the family, except for an annual invitation to hike around the Plitvice Lakes.

A third of the way through the diary, it became clear this was a record of my grandfather's final months. Undoubtedly, there were other volumes, stretching back through the 1980s and before. Though I feared these diaries had burned in the fire that overtook his house. Still, this one record contained enough of him, a man I had hardly known. I could take no more of his peculiar view of existence, and I left the office to clear my head. The rain had eased, leaving a glistening sheen on the pavement. I went to the café-bar on the corner and nursed a glass of Scotch, but abandoned the place when the television above the bar was switched on.

I continued my walk around the neighborhood flanking that side of campus. Some students were huddled together and talking of visiting the cinema. The arthouse was playing Kieślowski's *Three Colours* trilogy. I avoided looking in the doorway, lest I be tempted to remain in the warmth and the ocular glow of *Blue*, *White*, and *Red*.

Along the street, I bumped into a young couple kissing beneath a burnt-out lamppost. I apologized and moved on, ignoring the man's invitation for a fight and his calling after me, slurred words I could not decipher. Their affection for each other reminded me of my grandfather's descriptions of his wife's hands, the little drawings of her palms, the lines that resembled river basins. He quoted the poetry he read her at night: verses of Neruda, Mažuranić, some Verlaine. He had passion like that young man. I had none.

Close to midnight, I returned to my office and collapsed in the swivel chair behind my desk. I pushed aside the diary for my stack of vintage *Cahiers du Cinéma*, happy to see the familiar yellow borders and black-and-white cover photographs. In one, a suited Alfred Hitchcock, eyes almost closed, held up his hands to frame a scene. I flipped through the pages, touching the pictures and examining the captions. In my agitated state, little of the French made sense. I brought my vial of Xanax out of my coat pocket. I swallowed one of the pills, then picked up the diary again and began to read where I had left off. I rejoined my grandfather in his mapping of his wife's lines and scars, the knotted tissue above her pelvis, the birthmark that peninsulaed down her inner thigh. By dawn, I had reached a shift in my grandfather's obsessions. Transcribed radio transmissions filled several pages, detailing Serb movements a few kilometers from Voćin. Militia, some in uniform, most not, drove across the border, Kalashnikovs strapped to their shoulders. The men swarmed the village squares and Catholic churches, and they hung Serb flags and kissed the red stars of the tricolors.

For a moment I took in the brightening sky in the window. Though my mental coherence was intermittent, I knew these passages had been written weeks before my grandfather's death. I closed my eyes to rest from his words. When I awoke in the early afternoon, I brewed a pot of black tea in the faculty lounge and stole a packet of wafer biscuits from the cupboard. I ate a half dozen, and, somewhat renewed, hurried to my office. I edged around my desk, careful not to disturb the film canisters stacked atop my projector. Beside the silvery tower sat my boxes of teaching slides: stills from *Remorques*, *Le Trou*, a whole series from *Breathless*. Part of me wanted to forget the diary and revisit those films, perhaps write a new set of lecture notes, arriving at a series of hauntological insights on those masterpieces.

I sat in my chair again, leaning back into the leather upholstery, the deadening effects of Xanax leaving my body. I rubbed my eyes, then sipped a little of my tea, hoping the caffeine would hold me for a while. I creased open the diary and resumed my reading. The border towns and villages consisted of a mix of Serbs and Croats, a few Bosnians.

Voćin, according to my grandfather, had a ratio of 6:3:1. On one page he had drawn the badge of the White Eagles, a Serb paramilitary group. A number of these renegade soldiers had annexed the village. They had declared it part of Serbian Krajina, and they had set up roadblocks all through the hills. Before long they escorted several prominent Croats out of their homes and whisked them away in unmarked trucks. After my grandfather spoke of the illegal arrests at the village's café, soldiers dragged him to a shack in the forest. They asked him if he had killed Serbs in Podravska Slatina. When he said that he hadn't, they beat him with their rifle buttstocks. They left him in the dark for several days. Then, as he was old, they freed him on the condition of his silence. My grandfather moved with his wife into a friend's basement. Secretly, he continued to record the violence of the occupation. In spite of the threats to his life, there was little sign of bitterness in his writing. What I once assumed was his eccentricity I saw now as his awareness of history.

After scanning the entirety of a vernacular Shtokavian prayer, which had been copied into the middle of the diary, I noticed the handwriting had changed: once elegant and looping, the letters were now dense, smudged together. My first thoughts were a stroke or arthritis. But then I recognized the handwriting as my father's. He had carried on the observations and added in accounts of the massacre from sympathetic members of the village. The nature of the reports suggested he had visited Voćin. A few pages later, I confirmed my suspicion: my father had charted the positions of each slaughtered person in the village. Dozens of *X*'s dotted his crude map. An initialed M.P. marked the spot of my grandfather's death. I said his name aloud: Mirko Pavić.

Sometime later, I visited my mother. She wore a pastel yellow nightie half-covered with a tattered cotton robe, the lace trim along the collar frayed and stained by the grease of her night cream. As she ushered me inside, she asked about my classes and my research. The former were fine, even if I was distant with my students and slow on returning their essays. I had abandoned my work on Derrida and French film years ago—the field was vastly over-studied—but I still lied to her about researching the metaphysics of New Wave cinema for a book. It was clear during our talks that she wished I had a wife and child, people to anchor me to the world, to make me care about other things than the nature of reality in the films of Truffaut and Goddard. She blamed herself for my self-medication. Back in 1991, she had been the one who had identified my grandfather on the television. In those six seconds of video footage, she knew the body was his and told me at the time. The oval-shaped belt buckle had caught her eye—a past Christmas gift from her. I had never admitted to her that I had known from the burned remains of a pencil in his shirt pocket. How many old men in that small village would have had the same pencil habit?

In the living room, we sat and drank black tea. She had no wafer biscuits but she gave me a bowl of salted almonds, which I kept on the armrest and picked at now and again. Her house was small and cramped, and she had hung her washed dresses on hangers and hooked them onto the tops of the window blinds. As she shifted in her chair, her whole body was bathed in fuchsia light. I leaned closer to her, knowing her hearing was shot. I wanted to discover what she knew of the diary and my father's part in it all. After I asked, she raised her eyes to the ceiling and said my father had exhibited the signs of a failed writer—bitter, elusive, overprotective of the stacks of paper that she could not touch or move from his desk—and that play, she went on, was eighty-four pages of melancholy. She knew nothing of a diary. I do not want to know, she said.

I remained quiet while she relayed her fears that her husband had been a womanizer. She had scant evidence for this, just a single instance of him disappearing for a few days, and I tried to placate her with his last words to me: trust in the family. A smile broke out on my mother's face. I had allayed her anxiety with this fabrication, and I asked her about my father's parents, why we had never visited them in Voćin. To spare you the blood of the past, she said. She closed her eyes and spoke of my grandfather's final act: a return to the house. She speculated he went for something for his wife and perhaps he had presumed it safe because of the encroaching Croat force. Thousands of soldiers were coming to retake the region. Upon leaving his house, he had run into one of the few remaining Serb patrols. They had shoved him to the ground and gouged out his eyes with a knife. They splashed gasoline across his body and tossed a lit match onto his chest. My mother cried when she described the heroism of my grandmother, who had followed her husband and was made to watch him die. But she defied the shouts of the braying men and extinguished the flames with her shawl. My mother's voice was shaky, and she repeated the details of my grandmother's anger, her words to the men forced out through her grief. What have you done? she said. No one answered her. They fled Voćin as quickly as they had entered. My mother raked her fingers through her gray hair.

Her eyes were watery, focused not on me but something beyond her dress swirling in the breeze of the open window. The longer I sat there, in the clammy late-autumn heat, the more it occurred to me that my mother had gotten old. And so had I.

I do not recall now when I departed my mother's house. The timeline muddied, as it was, by a double dose of Xanax. Yet it occurs to me that I avoided the emptiness of my flat in favor of the five square meters of my office for a good reason. There, surrounded by my life's work, I attempted to fill in the missing architecture between the diary fragments, reconstructing a whole existence from the banal detritus. I tacked the pages to the wall opposite my desk. Each day I wrote four or five pages freehand, connecting the parts of my grandfather's life, understanding how he drew vitality from his wife and his interest in the village. When I added in my father's later additions, the map and the odd snippets of stream-of-consciousness, the text became a collage I could reference to form a stable narrative about our family. Perhaps more than a ghosted autobiography, it was a memoir of sorts—a joining of three generations of Pavić.

For a month or two, I attempted to make sense of this re-creation. The manuscript consisted of strings of words, barely sentences in the conventional sense, my prose more closely resembling an epic poem written in a language forgotten to history. Soon after admitting this to myself, I abandoned the approach. I drank less, ate meagerly, lost a few kilograms of middle-aged heft. During this bout of asceticism, I cleared the wall of the diary's pages and set up my projector, watching that segment of television news on a loop. Frame by frame I gazed upon the stiffness of my grandfather's body as the reporter removed the blanket, taking note of the slow warping of his expression as he pointed to the dark holes in my grandfather's face.

My life existed within this cinema of terror until the university sent a letter informing me of my teaching review (low-quality lectures, uninspired students) and my record of publication (non-existent). The letter served as a written warning. It noted finally that I had one last semester to make improvements on both fronts. Both my colleagues and I knew change was unlikely. My time in my comfortable university office was over.

Before winter break, I informed the chair of the department I would not be returning in the spring. He shook my hand and remarked he was surprised I had stayed so long. In my office I left behind almost everything, including a filing cabinet crammed with lecture notes and ungraded student essays. I lugged out my projector and films and the last packet of wafer biscuits from the faculty lounge.

Not long after this my mother called to say she had dreamed of my father and asked me to bring her the diary. When I gave it to her, she went to her chair and read all afternoon. My mother complained that she found the diary more incomprehensible than my father's play. Slavs want to believe they are special, she said, that they are superior. I felt unsure where she had come up with this idea. I tried to counter with what Derrida said about the incompleteness of representation and how it is adrift in time. Life has nothing to do with theory, she said.

Perhaps to prove my side of the argument, I took the

train to Velika the next morning and hired a car so I could reach Voćin. Ice had formed on the roads and the forest that engulfed the region had become a vast sea of shapeless gray. All those years ago, after the war ended, my father must have taken the same route, seen the scarred landscape and tried to work out how such a terrible thing could have occurred in his homeland. I remember during the studies for my PhD when I came home once. My father seemed aloof, distant from my mother and me. Smoke swirled around his face as he dispatched one pack of cigarettes after another. I could do nothing to save him from his thoughts.

Eventually, in Voćin, I drove past the piled stones of a mortared Catholic church. Half a wall still stood, now covered in graffiti tags. Farther along the street, the arrangement of the buildings was different to how I had imagined, and I struggled to find my grandfather's house or any landmark beyond the church and the village square. Knotted yews lined the roads and the cornfields. A couple of new redbrick houses stood on one street. I pulled over outside of a stone cottage and opened the diary to study the hand-drawn map. In the last light of dusk, I reoriented myself and drove south, toward the hills.

No one was around on my grandfather's street. Darkness shrouded the houses. Even so, I could tell most of the buildings appeared burned or half-demolished. A rusted bulldozer sat idle on the pavement. I recognized the street, the patch of cracked tarmac, from the six seconds of news footage. My grandmother once told me she could never watch that video or forgive the men who murdered her husband. Many of the Serbs who lived in Voćin moved out of the village, even before the war ended. In the years since several periods of reconciliation have come and gone, in futile attempts to heal psychic wounds, to put the massacred on both sides behind us.

I climbed out of the car and collected my case from the trunk. My grandparents' house appeared abandoned. The front door lay in two pieces on the hallway tile. Blooms of soot marked where flames had licked the walls and ceiling of the ground floor. A spray of bullets in the living room had pocked a dozen holes in the plaster. Up the stairs, I ventured into the front bedroom. A large mattress lay on the floor, half-covered with a blanket. I knelt and drew the fabric close, breathing in the old smoke. I threw the blanket over my shoulder, then opened my case and removed the projector and film canister. I mounted the projector on the windowsill, the lens facing out, tilted downward, forty-five degrees. I loaded the film reel and pressed play: the beam of light shot a sequence of murky images onto the blackness of the road. I paused the newsreel and went downstairs, carrying the blanket, unsure of how long the battery would last. Outside, I draped the blanket on the tarmac and smoothed the surface with the tip of my boot. As I stepped back, the still frame of my grandfather fully illuminated. He was lying on the ground. I could see the charred contours of his body, the slight angular twist of his final moments, all the pain he had suffered. I arranged myself into his death pose on the blanket, our bodies joined in the stream of light.

Acknowledgments

Thank you to the journals and editors who published these stories in earlier versions:

The Arkansas International: "Darkroom"
Consequence: "May Our Ghosts Stay With Us"
The Dalhousie Review: "Flight"
Day One (Amazon Publishing): "Men of the World" (as "In the Land of Lakes and Birds")
Epiphany: "The Distortions"
Grain: "Fatherland"
Notre Dame Review: "Zorana" and "Restoration"
Prism International: "All the Land Before Us"
Rock & Sling: "The Little Girls"
Takahe: "brb"
Witness: "Sojourn"

Thank you to the many readers of these stories over the years. To Erin Rose Belair, William Decker, John Dufresne, Toni Graham, Gabriel Houck, Alex Hughes, Nahal Suzanne Jamir, Denis Johnson, Rachel Lyon, Kelly Magee, John Mauk, Kate McQuade, Rick Moody, Aimee Parkison, Alex Poppe, Rachele Salvini, Eric Schlich, Randall Silvis, Caitlin Taylor, Brady Udall, David Heska Wanbli Weiden, Monica Whitham, and to the many workshoppers who offered me advice.

Thank you to my man, Keith York, for reading the collection twice.

Thank you to Courtney Sender for her insightful

suggestions and edits.

Thank you to Aleksandra Vujatovic for guiding me on the finer points of Yugoslavian culture and language.

Thank you to the institutional support of the Virginia Center for the Creative Arts, the Vermont Studio Center, the Atlantic Center for the Arts, and the Ragdale Foundation.

Thank you to the publisher, Luke Hankins, and his editors, Amber Taliancich and Jonathan Geltner, and to Samrat Upadhyay for selecting *The Distortions* for The Orison Fiction Prize.

About the Author

A former resident of Zagreb, Christopher Linforth is the author of two previous story collections, *Directory* (Otis Books/Seismicity Editions, 2020) and *When You Find Us We Will Be Gone* (Lamar University Press, 2014). Linforth's stories have appeared in *Notre Dame Review*, *Witness*, *The Arkansas International*, *Fiction International*, *Consequence*, and *Best Microfiction 2021*, among other places.

About Orison Books

Orison Books is a 501(c)3 non-profit literary press focused on the life of the spirit from a broad and inclusive range of perspectives. We seek to publish books of exceptional poetry, fiction, and non-fiction from perspectives spanning the spectrum of spiritual and religious thought, ethnicity, gender identity, and sexual orientation.

As a non-profit literary press, Orison Books depends on the support of donors. To find out more about our mission and our books, or to make a donation, please visit www.orisonbooks.com.

For information about supporting upcoming Orison Books titles, please visit www.orisonbooks.com/donate, or write to Luke Hankins at editor@orisonbooks.com.